M000166813

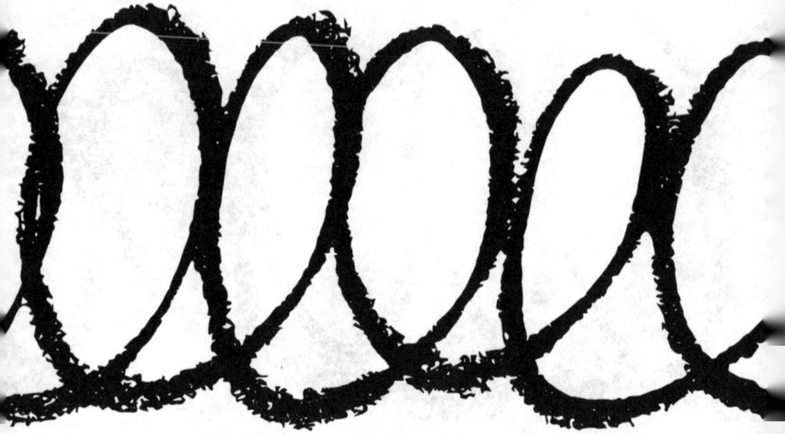

How to Adjust to the Dark

"In her debut novella *How to Adjust to the Dark*, Rebecca van Laer is relentlessly honest with herself and with the reader in the way that makes good writing interesting. She's superficial and raw and hurting and smart and out of control, and emotional and in pain and striving to find herself, to figure out, as Sheila Heti famously put it: how should a person be? It's a very personal exploration of the artist as a young woman, through a Salingeresque world of academia, therapy, prescription drugs, street drugs, failed relationships, poetry and self-discovery. I read it all in one day on a large desktop computer with photographs of Anaïs Nin and Edward Albee and Donna Tartt in my periphery. If only there'd been a photo, too, of Sylvia Plath on my wall, all would have been right in my world!"

—Elizabeth Ellen, author of *Person/a*
and *Her Lesser Work*

"A touching and resilient collection on art and desire, told in a hybrid of poems and prose—think: VH1 Behind the Music for Rebecca van Laer's poetry. Craigslist hookups, sunshine, pain, love and liquor and vomit."

—Bud Smith, author of *Teenager*

"I'm in awe of this book. In a fictionalized inner travelogue, Rebecca van Laer writes fearlessly about life, writing, love, and loneliness, with exquisite attention to detail. This is a book about the various forms of armour we wrap ourselves in—most especially the armor of identity—and about what we think we're protecting. This is a book about how big our desires are and how big we believe they can be. Like Maggie Nelson's *Bluets* and Sheila Heti's *How Should a Person Be*, van Laer takes so-called 'women's writing' and opens it up, showing us what exists beyond cliché and easy answers."

—Lindsay Lerman, author of *I'm From Nowhere* and *What Are You*

"In *How to Adjust to the Dark* the narrator seeks, grieves, and invents love in a series of vignettes interwoven with poems and literary self-analysis. This book is about the pain that comes with living by trial and error; there's really no other way to do it. I felt seen by Charlotte's relationship with writing. I couldn't stop reading, though I wanted to look away at times. Van Laer reminds us of how embarrassing and brave and beautiful it is to write, how our own words become life rafts. They are impermanent, silly, and wholly necessary."

—Shannon McLeod, author of *Whimsy*

Copyright © 2022 Rebecca van Laer

Published by Long Day Press
Chicago, Il 60647
LongDayPress.com
@LongDayPress

ISBN 9781950987207 (Paperback Edition)
ISBN 9781088021347 (eBook Edition)
Library of Congress Control Number: 2021952611

Edited by Nathan Stormer
Layout by Joshua Bohnsack
Cover Design by E.S. Mahler

"Do You Fear Palindromes, Too?" *TriQuarterly* 154, 2018
"Dorothy Comes Home from Work." *The Flatmancrooked*
    Slim Volume of Contemporary American Poetics, 2010.
"The Girl With the Red Hair Speaks." *The Battered Suitcase*,
    2009.
"Envy." *The Crab Creek Review*, 2010 Vol. 2.
"This Weight." *The Cimarron Review*, 169, 2009.

Printed in the United States of America.
First Edition

How
to
Adjust
to
the
Dark

**Rebecca
van Laer**

Long Day Press
Chicago

Chapters

Recently, my fortune cookie read:

> *All men should try to learn before they die*
> *what they are running from and to and why.*

This was the first fortune I'd ever seen written as a heroic couplet. And, while I know this message is mass-produced, I still feel it's a signpost as to what I'm supposed to do next. I don't think the universe is guiding me, but I use the detritus that comes across my path to guide myself. I read my fortunes and my horoscope, draw tarot cards, look at the moon, and wait for the moments when the signs in front of me pull me out of the present and help me imagine the future. This fortune tells me that right now (as before, as always) my future depends on my past, on all the couplets I wrote and then threw aside:

> I'd pull out my teeth
> just to spit them at you.

*

It's the first cut that lit me up—reminder
of the blood beneath the skin, the skin that
bleeds.

*

I do not want to be outside.
There is so much light there.

I have been wondering for a long time what to do about my poetry. Like this fortune cookie, the poems I wrote in my early twenties contain a lot of rhyme and aren't very interesting to anyone but me. Sometimes I've thought there is perhaps nothing to be done with them; they will sit printed out in a box under my bed until, like old diaries, they become so embarrassing I have to take them out with the garbage.

Like all young writers, I feared many of my poems were terrible as soon as I wrote them. Others are embarrassing only in retrospect. But some call out from the past in an uncanny voice, and it's hard to believe they came out of the same mind that I use now. When I read them, I can't remember either how I wrote them, or why I stopped. After a three-year deluge of verse, I couldn't bring myself to write a personal note in a birthday card, much less a poem.

It was difficult to admit that I'd stopped writing; I also didn't want to let go of my hard-won identity as a Poetess. *I'm just so busy*, I would tell friends. The truth was that I couldn't write anything new. So eventually, I had to start telling people, *I'm not a poet anymore.*

Gillian White writes that, since the 1970s, Americans have been *ashamed* of lyric poems. Ben Lerner describes poetry as "an art hated from without and within," embarrassing for both the poet and the reader. What is so shameful about poetry, exactly? Literary theory has stressed the impossibility of a coherent text, much less a coherent self. To be a lyric poet today—to say "I" and mean "I"—seems to depend on both the faith that a box of words can reflect *you*, and also the faith that you are definitely interesting and possibly important.

When I stopped writing, I had let go of the idea that I was important. And I was ashamed that I had believed I was for so long. But I'm not sure where, exactly, I began running from rhyming and writing. And so I decided to go back.

I'm increasingly interested in writing as what Michel Foucault calls "the care of the self." After retiring as a poet, I became obsessed with self-care in some of its more consumerist guises: buying moisturizers made with indigo and turmeric and snail serum, watching *The Bachelorette* to turn my thoughts off. I paid for yoga classes and acupuncture and ate superfoods. These are ways to care for myself, to maintain a healthy body and mind, and perhaps to even to heal past wounds. But there is a difference between "self-care" and the "technologies of the self" Foucault talked about in his late lectures.

Self-care is the maintenance of a healthy ego, while the care of the self may be painful. As Foucault defines them, technologies of the self-involve entering into an intimate relationship with one's past and present, often through writing. The goal of such self-analysis is not just to know oneself, but to "form oneself, to surpass oneself, to master the appetites that threaten to overwhelm one."

Such writing demands not just reflection, but the exertion of power to transform what is no longer useful. To look back, to be present, to reshape oneself for the future—this is no easy task. Yet in taking this power over the self, one learns to live more freely within the larger structures of power that are inescapable.

I've been afraid for a long time to look back at the rends from my past for fear of coming unwound again. But everything I come across tells me I am ready to examine this writing, and what came after. To make all of it useful again.

*

When I used to teach writing, I always began class with the same assignment: write a poem based on a myth. I encouraged students to interpret this broadly. Whether urban legends or fairy tales, myths can serve as a template for using surreal imagery to explore a speaker's emotions. This still seems to me a perfect way to begin writing. The hard part, after all, is making things up: people, their feelings towards themselves and others. To write a myth, you needn't develop new content, only locate the mythological character with which you identify most and write yourself into her.

I received this assignment in my first creative writing course, and it gave me the confidence to write poetry. It did not require the invention of new characters (at least not yet), only that I suffuse the world around me with my own thoughts and feelings. I could write about anything in this way: a short story, a movie, something my roommate said to me.

Doesn't all writing begin with the artist making up a myth about herself?

Soon, all of my poetry was about the people I loved

and who didn't love me back. Could my writing make them love me more, I wondered? (The answer was, for a while, yes, and then it was no.) The way I imagine myself at nineteen, I think of a girl who might write about Cupid and Psyche: she is captive, her lover is love himself, and even this is not enough. But in truth, I started with a poem about Little Red Riding Hood.

Little Red

She gets dressed in the morning
dons a cape in red
and walks a bit and sees him at the bend
(the moral of this story is, after all,
that she zhouldn't speak with strangers)
and at the bend he stops & says
(he can't take her here)
"Why not pick some flowers?"
And she nods coyly.
At her house, there he is again
a wolf, predator (or just misunderstood)
nonetheless she is there,
and I've heard that she took off all her clothes
and jumped into bed.
He bares his teeth and she screams for a savior.
(Can a hunter help her now?)

After the blood is spilled,
she sits shaking over the wilted bouquet
her own womb filled with stones.

"Little Red" is a character, but also me as I was then,
a young red-head wandering into the woods of early
adulthood. When I wrote it, I thought I was exploring
my own experiences of shame: the feeling of waking
up well-aware that the person in your bed does not
want to have breakfast with you. The feeling that
comes just after he leaves. In this version, it is the girl,
not the wolf, who ends up full of stones.

But I wonder about that poem's second voice,
which appears in parentheses. Does the sympathy in
this poem really lie with Little Red? The second voice
tells us this story has a moral: she made a mistake; she
should not have gone out alone. This story has a moral:
the wolf is misunderstood. This story has a moral: he
planned to take her, yes, but she is the one who invites
him home.

This is something that it is difficult for me to
remember, to admit, all these years later. When I
wrote this, I did not see myself as a fragile thing, and
did not want anyone to think of me that way. I had the
usual set of fears: that I would be lonely, that my love
would not be returned, that I would not succeed at the

things I most wanted to. And I had suffered by that point in my life. I knew what it was like to feel full of stones, to sit on the floor shaking. But, I was bold. In my actions I was fearless.

By my mid-20s, I was afraid to walk four blocks home alone at night. I avoided half the coffee shops in my city, reluctant to run into someone who had hurt me, or even someone I loved but didn't care to see. It took me months to get up the courage to invite the girl from yoga class out to coffee. That is not who I was when I started writing. Had it been, I never would have written anything at all.

*

At a recent wedding, a friend of mine reminded me of someone we all knew in college—or really, "knew of," a campus celebrity a few years our senior. We referred to him as "Eat Pussy Dan." It's impossible to forget this nickname, and I remember where it came from: a tattoo on his inner lip. But I had forgotten that I was the one who discovered this by going up to him at a party and asking if he had any tattoos. He had pulled down his lower lip to reveal a faded tattoo that looked more like CAT PUSSY.

I can't imagine talking to this person at a party,

asking him about his ink and then running back laughing to tell others about what I'd discovered. But I was different then. My friends remember me as vocal, irreverent, and sharp as a knife. I saw myself this way too. I didn't worry about hurting others. More than that, I was eager to kill any naïveté that lingered in my way of interacting with the world, to destroy any part of myself that was afraid.

So, in this poem, I suppose I am both the girl and the wolf. I am a girl who wants to take herself by surprise, to hurt herself until she is no longer Little Red.

I accomplished this.

O
Stone,
Be
Not
So

The day after the wedding, I went to dinner with my childhood friend Hannah. She'd been living in London for six years by then. Meanwhile, I'd made my way between snowy cities in the northeast. The last time I'd seen her was at a funeral, almost exactly a year before. We'd both flown back to the tiny town in Georgia where we grew up, back to everything we'd tried to get away from. That weekend, we had been black-out drunk on martinis, crying. We hadn't talked since. My Facebook messages went unanswered; I only heard from her in the form of a Christmas card.

A year later she was bubbly and wanted to hear what I'd been up to. I told her I was planning my wedding. She thought I was kidding. *You were punk by the time you were thirteen!* she teased me. *What happened to art? To rebellion?* She had thought I was like her: grown up, working, sure, but hiding my true self and tattoos under my blazer. I could understand why. I had been suspended from our middle school graduation for dying my hair blue. I had drunk Everclear and ran through the streets of the suburbs with my shirt off and tried to get on the roof of a moving car. I had done these things and written about them in my public LiveJournal—the source of many feuds and fights, and also the place where I wrote about my mother's rages. She read it and kicked me out.

As a young person, I had never felt accountable to someone else. By the time I moved away from Georgia and in with my dad at fourteen, he didn't have much of an idea of what I should be doing, so he overlooked it when I stayed out in New York City all night, and when I called home from a bus stop in the morning, hungover and asking for a ride home. Eventually, I got tired of that and found other ways to lead myself forward.

This did not make me feel empowered. For a long time, I was sad that no one told me who or how to be. I didn't really have a chance to reject advice, to make a self in collaboration with other people's ideas of the good life. Hannah's rebelliousness was rooted in the conservatism of our tiny Georgia town. I, though, was never really rebelling against anything. I was reaching towards one idea and another, waiting to find something to fully tether myself to.

For a long time, that thing hadn't been *art*.

*

In creative writing workshops, professors often tell you to *write what you know*. Willa Cather said that writers have all the materials they need by fifteen, and an instructor of mine went even further: she told us we had gathered enough experience to say something interesting by seven.

When I started writing poetry, I felt this to be in some ways comforting—I had the tools I needed—and in other ways disconcerting—the *last* thing I wanted to write about was what happened to me before I left for college. Why do people always want to know the details of abuse? To feel something; to experience empathy and feel proud of one's capacity for it; to know someone else has been more damaged. I once went to a Sharon Olds reading. She shared with the audience a review of her work: "Sometime during the Truman administration, Sharon Olds' parents tied her to a chair, and she is still writing poems about it." I can understand wanting to write about this, and to feel proud for having done so. But I do not want this to be my story.

So, in my first creative writing workshops, I tried to *write what I knew* as a journalist would. My poems took the place of my LiveJournal, and my present experiences became fodder for writing. I was living in upstate New York, so I wrote about flowers and stones.

When my dad visited me there during the spring of my sophomore year, it felt to him like a return. He had once dated a girl who lived in my town and eventually lost her. We drove past her house and the waterfall where he'd camped out on visits. I had the impression he was there to feel his own nostalgia rather than witness my present. He was oblivious to the fact that I was being pounded by the waters of my own young life: love and alcohol and longing and rejection.

Down Through Women

My father and I drive up past the winter
white Taughannock Falls.

His first romance: he hitchhiked down
this very road in the psychedelic summers
of his long-haired, long-limbed, long gone youth.
Drinks at the once famous Rongovian Embassy.
Three-day dirty campouts under foam-white rapids.

"I thought we would get married," dry-eyed outside
her old house with a new porch.
First heartbreak. His words. I am silent.

Iris City Limits

Not mud but clay: no scent of things
reused, enrichening.
Legend says the soldiers' blood
still runs in the soil of the South.

Our side of town, my front yard
covered the clay with centipede
grass. Green sometimes,
it moved underfoot like shredded paper,

secreting black and orange insects.
In summer, the sun glared,
green grayed, red hills of ants sprung up.
I'd kick them out across the lawn.

Above ground: gray. Kudzu nets shaped
the skyscape, left trees trapped
beneath its nets.
We stayed inside: every wife a wife or teacher,

husbands in their banks, businesses.
When it rained
it all went out—
the whole town black 'til morning,

when the asphalt woke up railroad-tracked
with timber carnage. We took
the long way into town, around
the downed maples, past the Baptist billboard:

"You think it's hot here?—God," past
the lawns of raked red, their families
sipping lemonade on the porches.
When a local airplane crashed

into the discount supermarket,
my parents tried to shield my eyes
as we drove to the air-conditioned
movie theatre. I'd heard the bang.

Now, I have a pink bikini. When I go back,
I'll sunbathe on the roof.

Reading this, I see that I had some sense of my privilege
as I wrote it: some sense of the deep racial inequality
that characterized the city I had lived in. The speaker
knows that while the lawns on "our side of town" are
green in spite of the sun's best efforts, the lawns on the
other side are raked clay. She knows that, while her
house is air-conditioned, other families' houses are so

hot that by sunset it's cooler outside. And she knows that this is something her parents try to shield her from. But she doesn't know how to write a good poem about this experience.

When I was young, an airplane did crash into the Piggly Wiggly grocery store about halfway between my house and Hannah's. It happened at night. The pilots, knowing they were going to crash, had diverted the plane away from more residential areas and towards a place where they knew they wouldn't kill anyone else. They both died protecting the town. In this poem, the crash takes on more meaning: it happens in daylight, and the force of it affects those who are shopping at a low-cost chain. The speaker has the luxury of driving past the scene of the disaster and going to the movies.

In this light, a few elements of the poem take on more meaning. The speaker does not explicitly say that the clay is actually truly red, only that "legend" tells us it is colored by the blood of Confederate soldiers. Griffin was a place where people proudly hung the Confederate flag. I knew how messed up this was. But the speaker does not indicate whose blood really pooled into the clay covered up by her parents' green lawn.

This can be a problem in poems: we spend so much time vividly rendering the visual elements of the world that we never get to why we should care about looking at them. Is there a worse way to acknowledge and take responsibility for one's own privilege than to sunbathe on the roof?

In writing this, I mostly wanted the object of my desire to imagine me in a pink bikini.

*

Through a haze of PBR and memory, it is hard to remember the specifics of this romance. Here is what I know: I met him my freshman year, the year before the poetry workshop. We both liked punk rock. He had taken a year off before going to college, which made him seem mature and worldly. He was a virgin and I was not. This made him seem less mature and worldly. I told other people about his inexperience; I went too far. He found out I had done so. He resented this. He dumped me, and we dated other people. I thought I had moved on.

During our sophomore year, I spent a lot of time at the apartment he shared with Daniel. We ignored each other for a month or two, and then in October we played a game of spin-the-bottle. We kissed everyone, and then we kissed each other some more in his bedroom. In the weeks after, I spent much of my time hanging out and drinking or watching something with Daniel and our friends Eloise and Rachel. Daniel always wanted to watch more porn, kiss more, feel free. Eloise was a spritely virgin who craved affection. And Rachel, with her blonde hair and eye makeup so dark she looked bruised, was the coolest, sexiest girl I'd ever met, always down for anything. I loved these friends, but I always hoped my ex would come home and hang out with us and get caught up in our games and laughter once again, kiss me again.

This happened two or three or several times. On one of them, I realized I was in love. On another, he told me we would only work in a vacuum. I might have made him a mix CD to try and convince him otherwise, and I might have given it to him. I know for certain that, one night, his small green and gray living room was packed with people. My beloved was smoking cigarettes inside, thanks to the freezing cold. I tried to drag him out with me onto the fire escape but he refused, so I sat on his bed and waited for him. When he came in, he told me to go home. "No," I said. "I want to talk."

He turned on his heel and left. The next time the door opened, it was Daniel. "Honey," he told me. "You should head back to your place."

But I wouldn't relent until he came back with a

tispy Eloise, who let me lean on her thin shoulders on the whole walk back to my apartment, where she slept in my bed. She knew this was the only way to keep me from going back in the night, knocking on his door.

A few weeks after that night, a squirrel entered my apartment and became trapped behind the microwave, screeching terribly. I didn't know that squirrels sounded like trapped birds, and I was afraid it might be rabid. I called my beloved to help me get it out— my place was on his route to our morning film class. He did so with his bare hands, and then we walked to the auditorium together.

During this period, I felt afflicted by forces beyond my control. A few days later, I broke open two eggs and found huge, orange double yolks in each. I took this, along with the squirrel, as guiding signs telling me that I must spend less time in my cursed apartment. I must go out into the world and *experience*. I must try to make something other than an omelet. All this is easy to remember for a clear reason: the squirrel and the eggs are vivid images, unlike the continuous stream of slights and reconciliations that make up so much of life, romantic and otherwise. I attached symbolic significance to both, and they stand out in my mind, bright against the mauve walls and linoleum floors of that apartment and that time.

The squirrel helps me to remember more. I was grateful to my ex for rescuing me from it and impressed by his bravery and compassion in guiding it out of the window. That compassion, however, was reserved for the creature. He was deeply annoyed that I'd chosen to call him, as he didn't have time to get coffee before class. So I was in love with him again, even though things were definitely over. Knowing what I know now, I see that I was fueled by the excitement of alternating between kissing and contempt. This would happen many more times.

*

A short poem about the need to unburden oneself:

Gossip

Oak tree, let me whittle my secrets
into your xylem, help me force
them into catkins and break them
into hardwood floors. I will eat
acorns by the handful, I will wait
for hours underneath your limbs
alone if you tell me how to talk
with birds.

My professor really liked it.

*

Knowing that my skills as a writer were growing, I wanted to prove my ex wrong about my "creativity," and I wanted to get his attention. I got it when I finally wrote a love poem, when I was unafraid of anyone snickering at my clear obsession during class.

As we had read more over the course of the semester, I became interested in something beyond description, beyond images like the squirrel and the yolk. What makes good writing? Show, don't tell is a mantra of the creative writing workshop (a subcategory of write what you know). We learn to describe with detailed images, and then we learn to build metaphors. Reading poets like Heather McHugh, though, I thought for the first time about the elements of language that do more than describe, elements that fail to signify. Rhyme, for example, doesn't mean anything, and once I realized that, it didn't become useless—it became interesting. This was to me for years the great mystery of poetry: why is it that the elements that contribute least to meaning contribute most to feeling? My fortune cookie illustrates this principle clearly enough.

All men should try to learn before they die / what they are running from, and to, and why. The rhyme helped these words stick in the back of my mind, the back of my mouth, for so long that I felt compelled to answer them.

This poem uses palindromes: words or phrases that read the same forwards and backwards. Racecar. Able was I, ere I saw Elba. A man, a plan, a canal: Panama!

Do You Fear Palindromes, Too?

Don't nod. I know you
place furniture off center,
unstack books and leave your pillows
at the edge of the bed, I know

your haphazard feng shui.
You won't meet my eye on level
planes, avoid my face. Don't tilt
your head at obtuse angles.

In parenthetical poses (bird rib
close) there is still, I swear,
enough space to shift. You move
a meter to the left, deny
the possibility of harmonic arrangement.

O stone, be not so,
I invite, as you stare
at the square door,
folding your shoulders into mountain peaks.

The title of this poem begs a question: what could be frightening about a palindrome? The first line responds with the poem's first palindrome: "don't nod." The speaker will be yielding palindromes as a weapon against her beloved: "eye," "level," "bird rib."

The beloved, the object of the speaker's address, seems hell-bent on leading a life of disorder. Are his messy living preferences—"unstacked books," off-center furniture—real, or a metaphor for destructive behavior within a relationship? When he doesn't look the speaker in the eye, is it because of fear of reciprocity, where the gaze between one lover and another is a living palindrome? Or is he just not that into her? The speaker's commands, her assertions that she knows him, straddle the line between seductive and delusional.

The third stanza of the poem is a plea: perhaps it *could* work. "There is still, I swear, enough space to shift," the speaker says—our love could be reciprocal and roomy. But the form belies a doubt: this indented stanza, boasting five lines instead of four, throws off the formal balance of the poem. He sees that doubt; he swerves away.

In the final stanza comes the final palindrome. "O stone, be not so" uses "O," the letter of poetic address to a person or object not present. Paul de Man says that this "O" tries to conjure up and even resurrect the dead, but it will always fail. Like a palindrome, the "O" has a function that is not precisely meaning making; it simply indicates that the poet is crying out to someone or something. In uttering this O, the speaker here veers into the histrionic, using a dramatic poetic device to capture the attention of her lover, to call him a stone, and to attack him with a final palindrome. It is not successful; he becomes even more stony as he folds his shoulders into mountain peaks. This final image takes the poem out of a bedroom and into a landscape in which words have lost their power and meaning.

I wrote this about the person I loved, and I am sure that, while writing it, I felt these tones collecting in the poem: coercion, delusion, desperation, pleading, resignation. The title, after all, is not "Do You Fear Palindromes?" but "Do You Fear Palindromes, Too?" The speaker does not suggest what she might fear about palindromes; perhaps this is one question I could not have answered at the time. But now I know. I feared living the same love story on eternal repeat: being together and apart and together and apart and together and apart. A palindrome has a beginning, a middle, and end, but the end is the beginning in reverse.

My instructor read this poem and was amazed by the transformation my writing had undergone. Her approval, mailed to me with a letter telling me that I should be a writer, transformed me into a person who believed she *was* a writer. In doing so, she gave me a gift, but also a curse. I had tried to win my ex back with writing, but instead, I had garnered my instructor's admiration. In doing so, I had learned that writing can be more than a tool to combat longing— when everything is risked, and when it is done well enough, it can sometimes fill you up again.

This is where the trouble started.

The
Girl
with
the
Red
Hair
Speaks

When summer came, my lease was up. I decided to move away from campus into a building downtown that was closer to the restaurant where I'd be working. Through the studio's thin walls, I could listen to the man in the apartment next door playing video games, watching TV, and grinding coffee beans. My furnished sublet had a big open kitchen and a tiny main room with yellow walls, a sofa, and a mattress tucked into the corner, right on the floor.

During the move, I pushed my AC unit right out of one of my windows, and it broke in the driveway. I didn't bother to pick its contorted body up.

I woke hotter and hotter every morning; the sun shone directly into the corner where I put my pillow. Sometimes I slept with my feet towards the wall. My cat slept in the bathtub to avoid the heat.

To mark a transition, I bleached my red hair blonde and began wearing it in curlers as I lay around the house, mostly on the mattress even though there was a sofa right next to it.

Years later at a yoga retreat, after practicing the

Ashtanga primary series and preparing for the first workshop of the day, I saw the woman next to me sprawled belly-down on her mat rather than sitting in lotus position. She turned her head towards me and told me she lived after Winston Churchill's motto: "Never stand up when you can sit down. And never sit down when you can lie down." I immediately crawled onto my belly as well, feeling my heartbeat against the ground.

That summer, I did no yoga, or any other physical activity. I had no excuse for sprawling in the sun like a cat conserving its energy—I just knew that my couch didn't seem like the right place for me. I took selfies on the floor; I watched TV on the floor; I ate with my feet hanging off my mattress onto the scratchy rug. Sitting on the sofa when visitors came over was a strange feeling. I showered over and over again, hoping the wet hair against my neck would keep me cool.

Eloise and Rachel were in Ithaca, living up the hill and going to bars every night. Having a fun time going out drinking and meeting guys, they became a pair, and then part of a posse I no longer felt able to join. My fake ID was much worse than theirs, and I could only go to one bar in my neighborhood, far away from everything else. So I signed up for the night shifts. I was working in the pastry division and I had a painful crush on my supervisor, a man in his thirties who showed me how to roll bread loaves of various sizes and shapes. He was good with his hands, quick to laugh, and made me a cappuccino on the one occasion he saw me crying. This was in some ways a good job; although it was hot outside and hot in the kitchen, walking into the cooler was like entering a different world. Plus I could eat free tiramisu. I talked to my supervisor about my love for sixties girl pop, which I frequently played when I was alone at the pastry station. He liked it too—Joanie Summers' "Johnnie Get Angry," The Angels's "My Boyfriend's Back." All these songs are about vulnerable women who love the toughness of the men in their life. A funny thing to listen to in the deeply sexist kitchen environment I was in. I was off in the corner baking, but it was impossible to tune out my surroundings. When there was a sudden rush, the sous chef would say to the male line cooks, "Hurry up, ladies. Do you need a tissue? Do you need a tampon?" The other chefs never said these things when my supervisor was around. I wished they had, so that he would hear it and speak up. I wanted to be protected, but it didn't occur to me to leave this situation in which I felt so uncomfortable.

I played girl pop in my car as I drove around. I

played it as I rubbed herbs on focaccia dough. And, listening to these songs about true love, I found that, like the women singing, I wanted nothing more than to fall in love. Maybe that would fix the way I felt. Maybe all I needed was a new fixation.

That summer, I would've said I wanted to find a companion. For years I thought that was what I was seeking. The relationships I found myself in proved otherwise, suggesting that what I wanted, really, was to feel sharply the cold of unrequited love. I did not yet know this. I did, however, know that my supervisor was not interested in me. I was, after all, an employee a decade his junior. I'd have to look elsewhere.

I went up the hill to a party. Brash, blonde Rachel had friends who were graduate students—older, but not too old—and she introduced me to one. A classics student, he was short and pale and vampiric, but smart-seeming. We had a picnic, playing croquet and drinking too much from the afternoon late into the evening. The graduate student and I flirted through the sunset, and then moved inside Rachel and Eloise's with a few more bottles of wine. At some point, we made our way to his apartment, where he put Tom Waits on his record player and served me another drink. We slept together. I felt like I had found my next boyfriend, my companion, immediately. Why shouldn't it work like that? (Why did I always think it would?)

The next day, my friends and I were driving to a music festival in the city. I hurried home in the morning to pack, hungover and anxious, excited and sick.

The drive was more difficult than we'd anticipated. Rachel was wrecked, too.

"Did you puke last night?" I asked her.

"No. But I guess I forgot to drink water."

"You two were wasted," innocent Eloise said, pointing out the obvious. She'd left hours before, 'to pack.'

We felt nauseous, we laughed high-pitched laughs, and I told them about the graduate student.

"How was it?" Rachel asked.

"Good," I said, even though all I remembered was the feeling of a hot body over mine and the heel of his hand making contact with my face. Once, twice. "Do you like this?" He had asked me. "Yes," I said, "yes," surprised to find that I did. So he did it again and again. I had a raw feeling between my legs, hickeys scattered across my breasts.

We stopped to pee at nearly every rest stop on the four-hour drive to Eloise's parents' apartment on the Upper West Side. By the time we arrived, my heart seemed to have stopped racing.

We left the apartment almost immediately for the festival and spent the rest of the weekend sitting in the sun. I was smoking cloves, hoping to cut back on cigarettes. Eloise had a friend who was interning at a record label, and he kept bringing us rounds of free beer.

I waited for the graduate student to text me and ask me how the festival was. He did not. The days were humid and blurry. I ate the yogurt and granola that Eloise's mom stocked. I slept in the guest bed with Rachel and woke up every morning feeling as if my lungs were filled with fiberglass. I wanted to enjoy myself and the music, but I felt like I was only half there. The other half of me drifted back to my phone again and again to check my messages; it hovered back across the miles we'd traversed. Was he thinking of me?

It took us two hours to get out of the city. When we reached Pennsylvania, it was raining so much that all the cars had to pull off the road for twenty minutes at a time. After more than an hour in the driver's seat, Rachel began to panic, so I took a turn driving. Eloise didn't have a license. But I felt panicked, too.

I texted the graduate student from a rest stop outside Scranton, asking to see him the next day. Sure, maybe lunch? he replied. I settled back into my body; I could finally breathe. Maybe it would all work out. Maybe he was just giving me space.

The next day, I met up with the graduate student before my shift. He let me know how much he regretted what had happened. "I was so drunk," he said. He was ashamed of his behavior. How was this supposed to make it better—this rejection?

I felt like I'd done something wrong again.

That summer, I felt my body leaking—sweat, desire, everything—and wrote about it. In *Eros the Bittersweet*, Anne Carson argues that it is inevitable that the first poetry was love poetry; as written language was invented, poets began to reach for the words to put down their thoughts. Both desire and writing "require the mind to reach out from what is present and actual to something else, something glimpsed in the imagination." The joy is in the reaching, not the grasp. She translates Sappho's address to Aphrodite in "Fragment 1," one of the first poems we know of in any language:

> …But you, O blessed one,
> Smiled in your deathless face
> And asked what (now again) I have suffered and why
> (Now again) I am calling out

And what I want to happen most of all
In my crazy heart. Whom should I persuade
   (now again)
To lead you back into her love?...

My heart felt crazy, and I couldn't stop writing about it. Reaching for the right words, the right person.

Sex, virginity, and menstruation are mixed up in many of my poems, as they are in our cultural imagination. Desire poured out of me, seeking a welcoming vessel.

The Girl with the Red Hair Speaks

1.

Autumn lasts
only one week here,
the poplar trees shocked
all summer by the egg-
frying heat, ready by August
to blush and cower.

So the rusty skyline tumbles
into the earth, so parched

the grass has grown gray
and sparse showing the body beneath.
The strata drips into one shade

before the leaves'
winter strip.

I'm still floating laps
in the aquamarine pool, grasping
towards the white walls, flooding my eyes
with summer's incandescent hue.

2.

I didn't know
what was inside of me
bursting or growing
what might fall out,
bloom upwards or wilt
if I opened my eyes,

left the pool's embryonic blue:

what would seep
if I didn't leave

five fingers pressed
to my stomach in my sleep.

3.

So much time spent
in the bathroom
with my face
cooled
against the paisley wallpaper
I became familiar
with every pore,
the veins in the palm,
the blood spoking out of an iris.

4.

In the night, in the night
I wake
they say
you can't die
in a dream
            I wake
curled knees to nose
and hair sticking
glossy, matted

to the nape
to the lids, to the lips
my fingers grasping
flesh and cotton.

What is it that pushes the red out of us?

The title, "The Girl with the Red Hair Speaks," and the final line, "What is it that pushes the red out of us?" suggest that the speaker's red hair has served as a precursor to all of the other shades of red that will come out of her: the blood that pumps through her veins and stains her underwear. The same force pushes the hair out and the fluids through her body. While writing this, I was glad I had gone blonde.

But even in the poem, change was on its way. The first section discusses the end of summer; fall is coming, and it will be swift. As she prepares for that change, she reflects back on her nightmares, and the time she spends in the bathroom. What has happened, bringing her to this point? Why is her face pressed against the cool wallpaper? Why did I spend so much of the summer prone, my cheek against the mattress and the jersey sheets absorbing my tears? By the final section, the nightmares seem to be over—the speaker wakes up, knowing that she has not died. Whatever she has lost, she nonetheless lives.

Like a
Doll

The following year, I moved into a new apartment with Eloise and Rachel. I painted the room a color called Art Deco Pink. I had what I believed to be the best of three bedrooms in the unit: with windows overlooking a few scraggly trees, I could hear the sounds of birds in the morning with the light coming in. Yet it was becoming difficult to get up. We all went to classes, then came home to eat our take-out and microwave meals together in the living room, starting to drink the wine that Rachel bought with her fake ID. We went to parties on the weekends, making eyes at boys and then coming home together, blasting "American Boy" and dancing on my bed. I loved my friends, but every Friday I felt keyed up with hope that something would happen to make me happy, to take me out of myself. Since I'd cast the love for my ex out of me, nothing ever happened. I just woke up in the morning hungover and crying. What was making me so sad?

"You just need to drink pickle juice," Eloise said.

"I don't think you can talk, Eloise. You don't get hangovers," Rachel rejoined.

"I do too. My head totally hurts."

"Charlotte and I both puked last night and you didn't. You're not drunk if you don't puke, and if you're not drunk, you can't be hungover."

By Halloween, snow was falling. On the way back from class, I slipped and fell down the slick sidewalk. My legs were always bruised.

Looking, searching, I alighted on a new love interest—a musician. I had sex with him twice and realized he kindled nothing in my heart, gave me no desire to pour myself out onto the page. Unfortunately, he felt differently. He wrote me a song and had several mutual friends play backup instruments on the recording. As I listened to it, I burned with what I first felt was a hot shame. But no—it was a fever. The flu. Then, I spent ten days in bed watching Gossip Girl. In the other room, my friends listened to the song on repeat and laughed. I texted the boy that I was in no shape to see anyone. I meant that I was physically sick. Once I got better, I realized I still didn't want to get out of bed.

I went to a therapist for the first time as a legal adult. I couldn't stop crying. I heard for the first time, "I think you're depressed." Before I knew it, I had seen a psychiatrist and started Zoloft. When I told a few friends tearfully of my new diagnosis, they told me that everyone goes through a period on antidepressants. I was not consoled.

That semester, I skipped half of my classes. I emailed most of my professors and TAs, first about my prolonged flu and then about my depression. They didn't know what to say. I made it a point, though, to go to one workshop focused on the modernist poem sequence. We read Hart Crane's *Voyages*, John Berryman's *The Dream Songs*, books by men who had thrown themselves off boats and bridges. The lyric poem seemed to me fleeting and inconsequential after I had read Anne Carson's *The Autobiography of Red*. I realized that poems could hold much more than I had imagined.

T. S. Eliot says, towards the end of *The Waste Land*, "These fragments I have shored against my ruins." I am sure this statement ran through the mind of every confessional poet—Robert Lowell, Sylvia Plath, Anne Sexton—as they wrote their major works.

In this workshop, I wrote "Like a Doll." It is hardly a major work, but I thought of Eliot's phrase often as I wrote it piece by piece.

In therapy for the first time, I was spending a lot of time in my childhood: in the room I lived in, in the state I lived in. There was nothing else to think about or write about until I'd gotten it out of me and into a neat container.

I began a poem with images from my childhood in Griffin, where I wasn't allowed to decorate my own room. It looked like the room of a little princess: rose patterned wallpaper, an iron bed stacked high with pillows, pink sheets and blankets. My shelves were filled with stuffed animals, and the one right above my bed was lined with porcelain dolls. When friends spent the night and we slept head-to-toe, this gave them an eerie view of the dolls, illuminated by my night light. The first time Hannah stayed over, she called home before dawn.

On my dresser were photographs of me as a child model, posing with a handsome man in his 20s who was supposed to be my father. We held hands and he kissed my cheek. There were once life-size versions of these photos in a salon. When they changed the décor, my mother claimed them, put them in the attic, and years later, when I'd moved in with my dad, burned them in the backyard.

I did not know what I would make from the soft detritus of my childhood, or what it had made me. I would have to let it unravel.

Like a Doll

1.

To build a body, equal parts stone and
cellophane
and stranger still, to kneel to it,
to alchemize one's own flesh—

first, collect soft detritus. Take
the downcast lashes from another
woman's grieving face, paint on pursed lips.

Think porcelain, think doilies, think only
like a fur stole, glue tulle from head to toe.
Keep those knees up off the grit,

never falter but in speech: stuff the head
with downy feathers, fill the mouth with
cotton—
demure can't be outdated or destroyed.

It's a shock these wrists don't break
under the weight of sewn-on lace and stolen
bracelets,
but even this is not enough—conceal

a core of timber. What's a body
that can't bend over backwards
or stand up straight when on display?

2. Typology

Of course there is a difference.
Some contain a strange hollowness.
The first bodies, the limbs seeming sturdy
but airy at the core. And the center soft, poised
at the slightest tear to spill forth and multiply
into snowdrifts. The heads we're asked to cradle
to our chests, the stitches visible
at the neck. A plastic patchwork,
a gruesome incongruity
between periphery and center.

3.

What did I name them? Better question:
when did I realize they needed names,

polished stone faces so unlike my own
with pleading eyes
that seemed to shift from side to side;

parenthetic lips that cannot lisp,
that cannot force out vowels,
respond only with ellipsis.

Skin opaque and matte, when held to the light,
so like a seashell, in its fragility

and when held up to my ear seemed
that they might murmur secrets from the sea

Charlotte, Charlotte, Charlotte—
I named them after me.

As the sections unfurled, I drew more on my own experience.

Until I was four, I named every toy that I received "Charlotte." I no longer have any of the Charlottes, only a stuffed pink rabbit named Heather. My dad tells me that, upon receiving the bunny, my parents asked me to really try and give it a name other than my own.

What would make a child name toys after herself? It seems narcissistic in the colloquial sense, and in the Freudian sense. Each person, according to Freud, begins as a narcissist, with the ego loving only itself:

"Loving oneself is the libidinal complement to the egoism of the instinct of self-preservation." However, the healthy ego begins to distribute its libido and develop attachments to other entities over time: to the mother, and eventually, in 'normal' development, to a romantic partner. To continue as a narcissist is, for Freud, pathological. I think of myself at four, only wanting to play by myself or with dolls named after myself—unable to love someone or something that was not *me*—and this seems very funny and also very sad. After all, I had two parents and a baby brother. Continuing to read this naming through Freud, Heather is the first toy I understood as separate from myself. That would explain why I still have her today. But that is not my reading—not my experience. As many times as other people have told me I'm self-centered (here I am, going down and down into my own poem), I know the truth is more complex.

The poem works towards an explanation for my problem with naming. The dolls described here are the ones that gave my friends nightmares. They are porcelain, but they seem like stone, totally inhuman. Although they are silent, their moving eyes suggest the dolls are not dead. Rather, they are not permitted to tell their stories.

The image of the doll becoming a seashell, cradled

against a child's face, seems poignant to me. Just as children listen to the sound of the ocean in seashells and mistake the rushing of blood in their own heads for it, children hold dolls to their chests hoping to feel something from the doll, when all they can feel is what is already inside themselves.

But in this poem, when the speaker holds the doll's cool face to her own it is not that the doll is like herself (lovable, warm) but rather that she is like the doll: pleading, silent. And so she names them, all of them, after herself.

This is how I begin to retell my story, and to make sense in this poem: in naming my toys Charlotte, I indicated my likeness to them. I did not imagine dolls as extensions of myself, living and breathing, but rather saw myself as decorative, mute, and helpless.

I continued breaking up these reflections on myself and my childhood.

4. Typology

Of course, there is a difference.
Sometimes, it's like being in a candy store.
The vibrant yellow business suits
small magenta combat boots
heels that match the leopard eyes

an evening gown, a doctor's guise
and stuffed inside their box, stiff limbs.
A plastic sea of shiny legs
bursting towards the surface.
Of course, some had to be dismembered.

5.

Skin. Stitched hair, pores, cutaneous oils,
cuts and bruises, scars and splotches,
white and yellow tinted dermis,

fascia. Muscles wrapped as tight
as spools, red and purple
tugging.

Skeletal, smooth,
a monotone tapestry, a knitting of vessels
weak and watery, carrying

from center to fingertip,
the blood, the need, the oxygen.
Only at the center,

beneath the glut and wiring
can one see: the bone, the white.
The hard core gleaming.

6.

Clutching a body to the breastbone,

it becomes clear:

to name is to know; to make is to own.

7. Typology

Lying at the center of the white
tissue in the disemboweled
Christmas box, she appeared
so fragile I couldn't think
of how to touch her. Every inch
of skin an opportunity to shatter.
A moment with that silken hair,
and then they put her on a shelf.
She's been there ever since.

8.

Balloon curtains have hung limp from the
windows
since before you knew the shape of wrinkles.
Smooth the shades down to the dusty sill,
block out the light.

Turn the fabric-covered picture frames
in towards the tissue box,
towards the rose-spotted walls.
Face them down onto the talcum dresser.

The satin sheets remain unlaundered—
never mind those wedding relics,
those oily pillows buoyed by the brass frame.
Underneath you'll find, fresh and breathing,

the lace, the tulle, the chicken wire,
glue, pins and needles, parchment paper.
Sit down. Get comfortable. Put a chair against
the door.

In these sections, we move from dismembered dolls
to an image of the speaker imaging her own body,
unspooled. Confronting the self as hollow as the dolls,
the poem returns to where it began: with commands.
Indeed, the poem is circular; the entreaty to "put a
chair against the door" could be the beginning of the
work of building a doll (begun in the first section).
Perhaps the poem has been an elaboration on why this
building is necessary: to supplement the unappealing
body of the fifth section; to create something you can

own, to take control.

Why put a chair against the door, though? Is it there to keep a danger out, or to remind the doll-builder to stay in and dig into her work?

I showed this poem to Rachel.

"So funny," she told me over the rim of her gin and diet tonic.

"You think so? You don't think it's dark?"

"It's part of your whole Betty Draper thing, no?"

"I guess," I said. I thought my vintage dresses and sad poems were more of a Sylvia Plath thing, but what's the difference, really?

I wanted to end my reaching (or so I thought); I wanted to find a way to feel content—loved. So I did what so many of us did in the aughts: I posted a craigslist ad. I gave no personal details and posted no picture. I advertised only my gender and my feeling of isolation and waited for someone to reply, to tell me that when they went to the farmers market, when they milled around downtown on a busy Sunday, they felt profoundly alone.

I received many responses like this. One was from someone I had taken a film class with, someone who had never struck me as particularly interesting, or particularly sad. (I thought these two traits were more or less the same thing.) I received one from someone I knew casually, someone who *did* strike me as interesting and sad, but whom I had never been attracted to; reading his reply made me disgusted with myself, as if I had read his diary. I didn't expect this post to make anyone, least of all myself, vulnerable. The promise of craigslist was a special one: to pick up a missed connection; to forge a new one; to reach out through an anonymous post across the white and purple space of a webpage and find a like soul reaching towards you—a like soul who wouldn't kidnap you.

One reply would change me. As soon as I saw his email, I knew I knew him: he had attached a picture. He worked at the campus bookstore. I had seen him at readings and, once or twice, at the bar I could get into. His response was not what I would have expected. He told me that when he was in a crowd, he was his happiest. Many things about this post should have told me we would make a poor match. His attached picture revealed that he was cruising craigslist for hookups. Beyond that, his feelings toward the world were so opposed to my own that reading what he had written made me feel angry. Who *wouldn't* feel lonely on a huge campus, I thought? He didn't. He felt elated. But, because I recognized him, and, more than that, recognized him as a fellow literary person, I replied with a picture of myself—and he recognized me too.

Not just the picture, but also the girl whom he'd seen at readings. He had not yet read my poetry, but it had begun to serve its purpose. The fact that I wrote it spoke volumes about who I was before I opened my mouth. And so we decided to meet.

Anchors Like Limbs

We went to a restaurant called The Lost Dog. We talked about ourselves, our goals. We both wanted to be poets. He had graduated two years before from another local university and twice applied to the MFA program at mine. He was waiting to hear back on applications. Still a junior, I had a year before I'd send out my first. I ate sweet potato fries and a veggie burger—I was still too young to order alcohol—and then we went back to his apartment and drank very cheap canned beer. His room wasn't what I would have expected for a writer. He had a sports jersey on the wall, plastic cups from baseball stadiums, and framed photographs of his family. There were Christmas lights strung around the room then and always; he loved the holidays. He turned them on, we kissed, and when he noticed there were holes in my stockings, he slid his fingers into them and caressed. He drove me home in his car. I don't remember the conditions of our second date, except that we met downtown, I was wearing lipstick, and, once again, we didn't have sex.

I had expected, both in posting my craigslist ad

and in selecting this particular respondent, that I would find someone similar to myself—someone who wrote and drank and cried and fucked, often in quick succession. I did not. I soon learned that he had had a serious girlfriend in college, and she was the only person he'd slept with. He'd been celibate for the year since, and he wanted to stay that way.

When he revealed this, I felt strange for having had so much sex and with so little thought. I had never felt guilty about it, and if ashamed, only for thinking I could do so without getting hurt—the time I kissed someone in a field late at night after a bonfire, we'd slept together, and then he'd asked if he should drive me home at 2 a.m. because he didn't do sleepovers. The time I'd slept with a good friend after a different game of spin-the-bottle in a pitch-black room and he stopped talking to me afterward. The musician and the graduate student and the other men I'd met late at parties or in bars. They stacked up obscenely against *one*.

He had grown up religious; I got that. I also got that it was bound up with other things: the sports paraphernalia in his room, the Christmas lights, a sense of the communal and the good that excluded the dirty things people did together in the dark. I didn't expect a writer to have that sensibility, but when

I found him I discovered a desire for something I had never wanted before. I wanted to be the cheerful girl he had always pictured bringing home. This runs so counter to the writing I have already examined that it seems implausible this want could spring up overnight, like a fairy ring of mushrooms, but it did. So, I stepped into it.

One of the first things we did together was write about the life of a female saint—Catherine of Sienna. I was in a food history course reading Caroline Walker Bynum's *Holy Feast, Holy Fast*, which tells the story of female saints who took fasting vows in medieval and early modern England. Bynum makes the argument that this was not some precursor to anorexia. Rather, fasting nuns took control over their bodies in a way that was generally forbidden in their culture. In marrying Christ and refusing to eat, they were transported into religious ecstasy, into a realm where they could make their own decisions regarding their embodied lives. I was interested in the almost mythological claims these women made: that they lived only on communion, or on nothing at all. Learning of my interest in these Catholic saints, my new love suggested that we both write about them as a sort of competition.

This Weight
After Catherine of Siena

Yes, cream once ran over my tongue.
It never tasted sweet: I remember
only that hunger stitched

a pocket in my breast. Imagine
suddenly, sugar's grit does not dissolve:
would you spoon it still

into your tea, waiting
for pebbles to stick, gristles
in your mouth?

It is like that with me:
the sight of an almond's skin,
are reminders of the scratch

of pits. To be filled at all with the weight
of a tree's hard-wrought flesh—
I could not.

Yes, on bright days, white bathes
the brows of the children. At the table,
they will spread butter

on the bread I baked last Monday.
They will still feast on the flesh
of the ewe whom I have fed

all summer through. Their fingers
grasp, their ungrown bellies unstitched.
Love is sweeter than wine

my father first insisted.
I know what is sweeter than this.
The first time I broke my teeth

on hardened bread
from the fingers of a holy man,
I was six: the pain

was sharper than any
squeezing from these four sets
of palms. This hunger

is nothing. I once glimpsed
the eyes of a man with a face
as soft as lambswool, lips

pursed in fury. His long fingers
made a sacred shape
as He stared through me,

into the pit, the parcel at the center
and hated it

but also loved me
for my bones.

I cannot feel empty: now
this weight is His, and my own.

There is no mistaking that, however much it is about Catherine of Siena, it is also a love poem. My new boyfriend told me that tercets are ideal for talking about God, composed as he is of three parts: the father, the son, and the holy spirit. Couplets, then, are good for talking about love, a relationship between two people. I took this to heart.

In the poem, Christ can see into the speaker's (Catherine's) heart, and he hates what he beholds—but loves "her bones." This could refer to the fact that she is human, and that all humans, despite their fallenness, are God's creatures. Or it might mean that she has "good bones," like a house that's a real fixer upper. Or perhaps he literally means her bones—these are the only parts of her that are *not* in a state of sin, and she must fast until the bones are all that is left. However one makes sense of this partial, fragmented offering of love, St. Catherine's position of absolute devotion is also one of empowerment; in giving herself willingly to *Him*, she affirms her own will. She is his ecstatic, starving sub.

This poem has nothing to do with my relationship with my new boyfriend as it was then. Or maybe only a little: I wanted to give myself to him. I no longer wanted to be a broken doll.

*

Despite his doubts, we had sex. He looked into my eyes and I looked back; I wanted to fall into him. So I did. The next morning, we woke up and went first to a diner, then to a book sale, then to a coffee shop where we did work and ate ice cream. I never wanted to get up from that table with our laptops and coffee cups and melting sundaes between us. When he dropped me off at my apartment, I cried the moment I got out of his car and walked to the porch, hearing my cat's mews. My new boyfriend was allergic to cats, so he never entered the apartment. We spent most nights at

his place, underneath the twinkling Christmas lights.
I came home and found the litter box overflowing, the
water bowl dry.

*

Albedo

I had wood-paneled walls a window
that looked on three elms and a cedar playhouse—
with the windows open it felt like living
in the forest.

I had a cat. I fell
in love, I left him most nights, alone with a bowl
and catnip hidden in a corner.

I would say I miss him if I could remember
but recall only
my own hands stretching in the morning,
when the light reflected the snow
through the windows turning the sheets to warm slats
and him pulling the curtains shut.

In the neighborhood Christmas lights winked madly
until midnight and after that, more black.

The cat sat at the window eyeing dust motes, the kids
by the playhouse waiting all day.
When I came back he rubbed his head against my legs
he wouldn't stop yowling.

Soon, he told me he wasn't sure we should have sex anymore.

I felt like my entire worth was bound up in his decision. Was I or was I not desirable enough? It was beyond me to understand that this was the wrong question, the wrong lens through which to think of his wish to be abstinent.

*

We broke up for the first time after a trip to Ruby Tuesday's. We sat down with our menus, and he ordered a hamburger, while I ordered salad.

"Want to split some chicken wings?"

"I can't eat meat from here."

His jaw started to clench. "Why not?"

I was interested in food and its semiotics after my summer in a kitchen and during my food history course. So much of what we eat has meaning. My identity was intimately bound up with eating the pies I baked while drinking wine and crying. My boyfriend's was bound up with Ruby Tuesday's. But why? How did that make sense? He felt guilty about putting his penis inside of me, but not about all the suffering and processing and marketing that went into the tiny packets of flesh that he wanted to share?

"I only eat local meat," I told him.

"Well, why did you agree to come here?"

"I don't know. I thought you'd order one of those giant margaritas for us to share."

"You know this is my favorite restaurant."

"It's not a restaurant. The ingredients come from a warehouse. It's glorified fast food."

"That's not true."

But I couldn't help myself.

We sat at the table in silence. I got out my iPhone to check my email.

"God, who spends that much money on a phone?" he asked.

Now I was pissed too. We ate a tense dinner. But back at his apartment, I wanted to make up. I sat next to him on the bed, putting my hand on his crotch. That could fix it, if only he would let it.

He did not. He told me we couldn't see each other anymore. Our values were too different.

*

We had had a fight over seemingly minor things: my disapproval of Ruby Tuesday's, his disapproval of my iPhone. I felt galled, yet also sad that the *almost perfect* thing between us suffered from this complication: our different relationships to capitalism and its objects.

God, I didn't know that he could make me feel pain like that.

I wrote him email after email, and he responded to them all—never a good sign. We wrote back and forth, three or four times a day, trying to sort out our feelings but agreeing not to see each other.

I told my friends that we had broken up, and they told me good riddance. Daniel and Rachel warned me a hundred times that things with my boyfriend were ill-fated. Sex was important. Did he even like me? Did I even like him? But even if I had been told a thousand times in a thousand different ways—spelled out in notes, shouted in my face, written in the stars— it wouldn't have been enough to convince me.

Suddenly, I made myself scarce: I was "studying," I told them, "catching up." I didn't tell them about the emails. I didn't tell them that, ten days after we had broken up, we went to see an X-Men movie together, and then I sat in his car crying outside of my house for a second time. I didn't tell them that we met up in the public library and kissed in the elevator as it went up to the second floor. I didn't tell them that I was trying to win him back, trying to get him to sleep with me: if he decided once again to fuck me, I thought, he would have decided once and for all that he wanted our relationship, and that that meant compromising his idea of purity in a more permanent way.

I felt libidinally surcharged. I felt more strongly in love than I ever had before. And I felt angry. I wrote about these things in poems that are opaque, perhaps because of their shyness about being explicitly sexual, but also because this combination of emotions is so confused it is impossible to imagine them with even a little distance.

Anchors Like Limbs

> Things in their right place:
> gulls in the sky, salt
>
> on the skin—the mouth
> full of ocean, foam hands
>
> stroking the body as softly as
> a lover's first touch—rush
>
> and push into first whiplash,
> knees in the sand.

I've tried to hold on tightly,
invert this flood

to fill myself with subject—
but substance slips

from my palms as swiftly
as skate's eggs on the waves.

Fear of height, fear of water
fear of filling the body

with a souvenir that sinks—
I can't close my eyes when the tide rushes in.

This poem about anthropomorphized anchors begins with the narrator on her knees at the beach as the foam caresses her feet, her legs, her fingertips. This caress seems to turn immediately into a crashing wave, pulling her under.

The ocean is more than a metaphor for helplessness; it is a real cause of it. When I was young, I learned what to do in a rip tide: swim parallel to it, not towards the beach. It may carry you far, far out, but you will only exhaust yourself if you beat against it. Once you've escaped, approach the shore at an angle.

The speaker with her knees in the sand knows her powerlessness in the face of the ocean; moreover, with her knees in the sand she is "in her right place." This is the position in which women—at least in porn—give head: knees down, something salty in their mouths. This image may not be clear in the poem; perhaps I find it there because I remember the time when I wanted it there. On her knees, the speaker proclaims that she will reverse the tide of power, "inverting the flood" so that it no longer washes over her, but is contained within her, filling her.

She tries to fill herself with subjecthood, to gain agency. But she fails; everything slips from her hands, and the ocean drags all her hopes back out to sea.

*

In the original version of "The Little Mermaid," the Prince does not choose Ariel. The sea witch warns her well in advance that she will dissolve into sea foam if he marries another. At the end of the story, however, she meets a different fate. Having suffered so much in her love for the prince, she is rewarded with an immortal soul and becomes a cloud. She will shed tears for three hundred years before ascending further still and going to heaven.

The speaker in "Anchors Like Limbs" could be Ariel, realizing her stupidity and trying to find her way back into the sea but anchored by her new limbs. This version of "The Little Mermaid"—the mermaid whose heart is broken, who suffers, who dies—is one I revisited many times.

Shipwreck

At night, ships need light
to guide them shoreward. The wrong glow—
a lit window, lantern swung
from a stick by some treasure seeker—
sends the captain straight into a sandbar.

In the winter, I walk to the beach
each morning. The sun rolls, the waves shine,
the sand's still white and specked
with more shells than in summer,
no children filling buckets

with mussel shells, mermaid purses.
Ghost crabs scuttle out from caves, stop
as if shocked by the light. Gulls fight
for scraps of food.
No one else stands on the sand.

I sit on driftwood, inspect the stones
I've come to collect,
and place one on my tongue—the taste,
but not the texture of wet skin.
Oh, to be the happy foam

touching his feet! thought the mermaid
of her prince, and then she was. I think,
Oh, to be like him—
stepping on shells, sticks, her
last breaths diffused in the tidal spray — blind
but to the lighthouse shining in the distance.

Later, I simplified it:

After Taking a Walk

I forgot for a moment what lives
in my shipwrecked heart.

I did not want to be the princess, toppled by the
tide. I wanted to be the prince: the prince has all the
agency and power; the prince need not fill himself
with anything. And, at the same time, I felt like I
had gone off-course from this possibility. The story

about lighthouses from "Shipwreck" is one I heard during my childhood beach vacations. Off the coast of the Carolinas are the highest sand dunes in North America. No one knows why they are there; they may be indigenous burial grounds, or perhaps they are a natural phenomenon.. Hundreds of years ago, pirates stood at the top of these high dunes holding lanterns, and cargo ships looking for safe harbor mistook them for lighthouses. The ships crashed into the sand and their treasure was plundered. But there was no way to avoid it; a lantern and a lighthouse look the same at night, and by the time a ship is on-course for a dune, it is too late to turn around. Shipwreck is inevitable. Now, centuries later, the dunes are just another place for tourists to fly kites.

I had been shipwrecked. I was on course to find a wholesome love but ended up coming apart. And worst of all, my shipwrecked heart could find solace in nothing but the person who had rejected me. I wanted more than ever to be what he wanted. I saw no clear way to do this and stay myself.

It was not lost on me that this is the stuff of the earliest poetry.

All Touch, No Skin

We got back together. He'd made a final decision about sex, he told me: because he loved me, we could fuck without guilt.

We made this decision as winter break descended. The city was coated with a blanket of snow and everyone got out from under it. He headed west, and Eloise drove me south to my dad's house with the cat, Mister Suzuki, mewing in a cardboard box in the back.

I never liked going home from college. Its status as "home" was shaky. I felt it was really my stepmom's home, into which my dad gradually moved himself. I came a year later and slept on a futon in the basement, surrounded by Thai silk blankets to give me privacy from anyone who walked down the stairs to use the washer, dryer, or microwave—inconveniently located just near my bed, where I could hear footsteps and smell the Annie's Organic Burritos as I tried to compose texts, emails, poems. This was far away from the princess room in "Like a Doll"—not that I wanted the porcelain dolls, but I would've liked a door that shut. Eventually, the basement was finished, and I moved into a room with a tiny window in the corner.

But I still felt like a trespasser. I escaped the house at every chance I could—to go to Planet Fitness and run on the elliptical while watching TV, to go to a yoga class, to wander through the shoe section of Marshall's. I was already trying to lose weight, to look girlier, to become someone he would never want to leave again. I didn't go out socially, because I didn't have any friends there.

I called my once-again-boyfriend often while lying under a stack of blankets. Neither of us had New Year's Eve plans, so we decided to watch *Mulholland Drive* together with our phones cradled to our ears hundreds of miles apart. This was, in retrospect, not a very romantic choice.

*

When we got back together, I was so accommodating. He was sacrificing his beliefs to be with me. My desires had been the source of all our problems in the last incarnation of our relationship, I thought. In this one, I wanted to compromise as much as he had—or more.

He was a runner, so I began to run, both to participate in something that he loved and to begin to look like someone he *could* love, thin and athletic. I began on the treadmill and, when spring came, moved outdoors. Soon, we would run together through the woods on the north side of campus. At the end of the trek, I'd lean against the rough bark of a tree, panting and chugging water while he went three or four times around a large pond. I didn't have the stamina.

*

Depressed people don't get much done. But who cares? Productivity is overrated, really just another one of capitalism's demands. W.H. Auden writes:

> Everyone in his heart of hearts agrees with Baudelaire: "To be a useful person has always seemed to be something particularly horrible," for, subjectively, to be useful means to be doing not what one wants to do, but what someone else insists on one's doing. But at the same time, everyone is ashamed to admit in public that he is useless.

For a long time, I had enjoyed being useless—phoning it into classes, and only summoning energy and momentum when I needed them for a task that truly mattered. But now, my boyfriend questioned the fact that I took Zoloft. Questioned why, if we spent two days apart, I spent the whole time in bed with my cat watching *Law & Order*. Did people really need drugs to feel better? Exercise was a natural mood-lifter. Work lifted the spirit.

I tried harder. I studied and I wrote and I ran. He liked basketball, so I watched basketball. We went to odd sports bars and split pitchers of Budweiser. I ordered ice cream sundaes and ate spoonfuls while watching the game. These activities were not helping my weight loss, and neither were the antidepressants. I stopped taking them.

My friends kept asking me where I was, where I had been, what exactly was going on. I shrugged.

At times, I felt like I was happy-ish—happy to be pleasing him, happy to know what was expected of me. I told him I wasn't as depressed anymore, but I did not stop crying. It was worse, even. I was hungry all the time. Often, I kept my tears to myself, crying in the bathroom, but sometimes it started in public and I couldn't explain, couldn't stop.

He was not a fan of crying. He became very, very quiet, as if to pretend that he was not in the room—or as if to pretend that I was not in the room, and that he was deep in thought somewhere far away from me— so that I had no one to talk to. I cried harder and harder, and eventually he got angry. We tried to talk through this difference in disposition in a number of ways. I wrote a poem for him.

Thinking with the Skin

To know, meaning, to put two
fingers on someone else's lips
and think you feel

what they feel.
Meaning, to have a body
and to also be in someone

else's body—yes. I am
afraid of this, it is all
tongues and fingertips.

What I'm trying to say
in the space between my lips
and *kiss* is

this is all static.
Meaning, flesh is deaf
and dumb too. If you can never

sense the sense of the thought
that comes before this,
we have kissed into a corner. The mind

holds pain in hidden places.
I press my fingers to ribs
and can never find

the precise place the needle pricked.
A knot in the nape of the neck,
a splinter still in the space

between skin and bone.
There are two
ways of knowing things

that can't be seen:
I can tell you what you'll find there,
or you will grasp towards it.

This now strikes me as incredibly sentimental and cloying. This poem is about how "carnal knowledge" doesn't lead to intimate knowledge. I entreat my lover to try and know me intimately; that I can tell him where I hold pain and why, or he can ask me.

I assumed that he *wanted* to see all of me—that love is, in fact, complete and unconditional self-revelation. That once he fully saw me, I would finally *feel* loved, that all my pain would lessen.

I didn't know, then, that telling someone the source of your pain doesn't make it any easier for them to cope with your display of it.

*

I wrote a poem about a woman jumping out of a window that might reveal a lot about how I really felt, despite what I said to him, to myself, and to the therapist I abruptly stopped seeing in March.

Round Robin

Features blurred as brush strokes
in the distance between balcony and sidewalk,

she is wavering
like color on water.

Cracked light of her chest and limbs,
chin resting on the wind

with breastbone forward
like a robin perched on a rail.

...

I hate to say it but I never did like it much when
he put two fingers in my mouth and stared at me.
Still don't. His touch like a paper cut.

...

And then it happened: a release
like the separation of the yolk
from the shell, melting into the palm.

...

A shuddering running over.
A caress that can't be
as soft as thumbprints on a lover's lips.
You float and flutter. A wing
struggling against a clear weight.
This force without a body:
all touch, no skin.

The two lines describing the wind are the most interesting to me now: "This force without a body: / all touch, no skin." These lines are about the wind, or at least that's how I remember them. But they could just as easily be about whatever has driven the woman to jump in the first place—the relationship that afflicts her not through huge wounds, but through a series of accidental slights that sting and sting. This describes the force I felt: it did not emanate directly from my now-again-boyfriend. He did not encourage me to act differently around him or around my friends in words. But, afraid of losing him again, I internalized his habits. I ran more and more. I drank more and more. I went out with my friends less and less. After we had been together for four months, Eloise looked at me getting ready to leave in a tight olive-green dress and remarked, "You're vanishing." I took this as a compliment.

*

My boyfriend did not get into the MFA program. At the end of the spring, he went home for the summer, wanting to spend as much time as possible with his family. "Why can't you stay?" I asked him.

"You can visit."

"But I'll miss you so much."

"Don't you get it? Family matters to me."

"Don't I matter to you?"

"God, this again. You're like a black hole. You can't be filled up."

For a few days, he was not my boyfriend anymore.

I went home from a party with someone else. "Why do you stay with him?" he asked me after hearing the story of our on-again-off-again romance. I cried in his bed as he pretended to sleep.

I know I have to end it, I said in text messages to my friends. I knew how miserable I was. I was ready for someone to really love me.

Then, a text message from him. *My life would suck without you.* A Kelly Clarkson lyric and an affirmation that he wanted to be together again.

I had recently read Roland Barthes' *A Lover's Discourse*, and it seemed to echo all my feelings. The book is an encyclopedia of the terms that make up the feeling of loving, especially in an unrequited, longing way. In English translation, the terms discussed include "absence," "waiting," "anxiety," "catastrophe," and "will-to-possess." Barthes explores these terms in a book that is part autobiographical narrative, part literary analysis, part exploration of ancient and modern philosophy, psychoanalysis, and religious thought.

One could consider this a contemporary example of the ancient Greek 'Hupomnemata' Foucault identifies as a form of "care for the self": an attempt to know and define the affects that afflict oneself in order to free oneself of them.

Under the chapter "écorche/flayed," Barthes writes: "I am a mass of irritable substance. I have no skin (except for caresses). Parodying Socrates in *Phaedrus*, one should speak of the Flayed Man, not the Feathered Man, in matters of love." Barthes, in his project of establishing the "Image-Répertoire" that makes up the story of love, places the Flayed Man as one of the many figures for the lover. This is the lover who is sensitive to everything—so easily wounded, so prone to tears, so sensitive that he is the very opposite of thick-skinned: skinless. Every nerve is not only exposed, but also already raw, already flayed. And this flayed skin is not a result of the beloved's actions, but a result of self-torture.

I remember feeling raw. Just as much as "all touch, no skin" refers to the non-physical forces I felt to be exerted on me, they refer to how I felt. My poems established their own set of images in which I tried to express this feeling of woundedness without exposing too much. After all, I shared them with my now-again-boyfriend. My writing became very different in this effort at communication. The explosive force of my emotions was contained by my new routine; I tried to avoid this feeling of skinlessness by behaving as a model girlfriend. I no longer took my top off at parties or did whippets. I ran and I wrote. And my poetry, too, became more regular, more restrained.

Unsurprisingly, I was interested in cameras; they became a central part of my own Image-Repertoire. I took so many pictures in PhotoBooth during these years of my life, pouting into my screen. I was interested in looking at myself, and imagining how others looked at me. Cameras are obviously enough about capturing yourself as you want to be seen. In my poems, I am frequently trying to capture *someone*. This is, of course, a great tradition in love poetry; the coherent form of the poem suggests that love can be written down and immortalized. The subject matter of my poems—my continued attempts to write my love—attest to this belief in poetry. But they also convey a feeling of absolute helplessness in the face of this task.

At the end of that summer, I went to visit his family. I flew there; we were to drive back together in his car. I wrote about a moment on our trip:

Camera

From above, the whole state is sewn like a patchwork
　quilt,
fields of crops cut by seams of roads and rivers,
　impossibly
regular. This park is built to frame the place where
　three rivers coalesce,

brown water flowing. The sun swells down on the
　city's green
geometry, squares of ferns, weeping willows. From
　the wooden bridge
above the water, the city buildings look caught in the
　treetops.

How does it look when two rivers meet? They may
　then be one
merged in embrace—or two opposing flows, always
　beating
against each other. Here, though, the waters carve
　the park calmly.

A breeze stirs the brackish surface, the willow's limp
branches; lamb smoke rises from a nearby barbecue.
On the bridge, you take my picture, then I take yours.

The poem is about geometry: it begins with an aerial view of the Midwest and zooms in on a park. The "impossibly regular" geometry of the state is present in the layout of the park itself, and in the magic of three rivers, whose flowing bodies of water come together calmly. Everything here is regular, as are the stanzas of three lines. The poem takes most of its time acting like a camera; then, a literal camera emerges in the final line.

There is symmetry in the lovers' gesture: they each take one picture of the other. But they are not together in the picture—neither merged in embrace, nor beating against each other as two rivers might. They are simply disconnected. And on re-reading with this final line in mind, this disconnect reverberates in each image: the regularity of the landscape is "impossible" to fathom for this speaker; the trees around her are weeping willows, and their branches are limp. The smell in the air is not just smoke but lamb smoke, so it seems that something has been sacrificed. What, though? The camera's picture of their world is blurry.

*

At the end of the trip, he told me he was staying.

"For how long?"

"I don't know. Forever. I'm not moving back."

"What about your stuff?"

"I'll get it when I drive you back."

"It won't fit in your car, you know."

"It's all crap, anyway. I can just leave whatever doesn't fit on the sidewalk."

"Did you plan to leave me out on the sidewalk, too? Why didn't you tell me as soon as you knew?"

"I didn't want you to make a scene."

But I did. My eyes were rimmed with red at the last dinner with his parents. They tried their best to ignore me and the obvious anger on his face.

The next morning, we drove east, stopping places I don't remember, all the way back to our city, where we broke up for the final time.

Upon our arrival back in town, we went out for dinner. We were hungry after a day eating nothing but the tangerines his mother had packed, the hummus we'd picked up at a rest stop. Looking at the menu, I started to cry. And my crying in front of the waitress made him angrier and angrier as we sat and shared a quesadilla. He put cash on the table as soon as he finished and then walked out. I followed him down the street and tried to grab his hand. He yelled at me to never touch him again.

"That's why your mother's in jail," he told me. She was; although I hadn't spoken to her in several years, my dad had let me know. To be compared to her when I brushed his wrist—this woman I tried never to think about, this woman who had broken someone's nose—

It's still the cruelest thing anyone has ever said to me.

We speed-walked back to my apartment, where he'd parked his car. I cried and panicked and turned red; he got angrier and angrier. Once again, I was outside my house crying while he opened the door to his sedan, then drove away.

Even this was not the end: he texted me all night from his apartment on the other side of town. *This isn't about you, why do you make everything about you, why can't you support me?* I went over to Daniel's.

"You're lucky he's leaving."

Was that true? "But I love him. I don't want him to."

"You might love him, but he's not making you happy. Once he's gone, things can go back to the way they used to be."

But before him I had been sad, too—sad and directionless. With him, at least, I had had a purpose: winning his love.

My now-again-ex-boyfriend knocked on my door the next morning with a sunflower in-hand. He came inside despite Miser Suzuki's presence. We hugged each other and cried and lay in bed talking about how much in love we were for a few hours, and then he drove back home. That was the last time I saw him.

He was gone. All touch, no skin: in my room by myself, I felt broken open.

Apologies

In the wake of his departure, I was a mess.

I had finally turned twenty-one over the summer, so I went out dancing with Daniel. I wore all my single-woman clothes: a tube top with a lace panel; a tight, high-waisted pencil skirt; heels. I straightened my hair. Daniel danced with another man in the corner, and I became very bored and very drunk and the bouncer told me that I shouldn't walk around wearing outfits like that. I took this as a come-on and followed him around all night. I woke up the next morning in Daniel's bed, wearing his pajamas. "What happened?" I asked him.

"We had fun," he told me.

Classes would start in a week. I distracted myself by drinking wine and watching *True Blood*. I wished I had a vampire for a lover.

In the years before that, I'd been afraid of drugs. I worried that I would turn out not only depressed but also bipolar. Perhaps the occasional surges of creativity I'd experienced were early signs of a hypomanic condition. So for the three years prior, I'd never joined my friends in taking molly at a party, or doing coke during a game of *Risk*, or microwaving ketamine just because.

I wanted a change, though. This is such a common desire after a breakup—to be different, to change one's hair, to become vegetarian or get really into CrossFit or salsa dancing. I had already changed my hair, cutting blunt bangs in the bathroom. But now, I went to a party with my friends and did coke for the first time. I ran around the room talking to strangers. One of the host's neighbors came out while we were downstairs smoking. He told us to shut up and end the party. Daniel drunkenly warbled, "Do you know who I am?" Daniel was no one. I was no one. But we were young and high, and suddenly I saw the appeal. For a few sparkling hours I felt somehow significant.

Once school started, I returned to a routine. I walked up the hill every morning, then smoked a cigarette at the top. I went to the cafe in the library and sat down with a coffee before my morning class, then watched the other students pour in and out. I went to class and tried my best to pay attention. At the end of a long day, I went over to Daniel's. Eloise and Rachel were annoyed by my long absence, the drama and heartbreak, and besides, they both had boyfriends now. They were never at home. So Daniel and I drank wine and watched TV and, on the weekends, went out to bars more than parties. We danced to "Bad Romance" and did whatever drugs he had. Sometimes, he went to the city for the weekend, and then I sat alone in my apartment, waiting for my roommates to come home.

I kept running.

I started going to therapy again. I lied to my therapist about mostly everything: how much I drank, if I did drugs, how often I worked, how good I felt. But I was honest about one thing: I woke up every morning filled with rage. I thought about my ex, about everyone who had hurt me, and I felt a tightness in my chest, halfway between a scream and sob, before I opened my eyes. Sometimes I got up and started crying immediately, sometimes I got up and started to listen to songs on repeat: La Roux's "Bullet Proof," Christina Aguilera's "Stronger." But I didn't feel stronger.

My therapist asked me, "Would it be the worst thing in the world if you woke up that upset every morning for the rest of your life?"

I realized that I could indeed live with this feeling as long as I spent the rest of the day reaching beyond it.

*

I had started working on a novel-in-verse, based loosely on the characters from *The Wizard of Oz*. It would have the voices of Dorothy, the Cowardly Lion, the Tin Man, and the Scarecrow. The Cowardly Lion was Dorothy's lover. I mostly wrote parts for the couple. I read some of them at an issue launch for a student magazine, and a graduate student, drunk and flirting with me, mapped out the themes of the poems on a napkin. I was surprised to see him list "alcoholism" and "abuse" among them. He kissed me on my forehead before I went home. Eloise told me that the man had been in a seminar with her—he had a wife and kids. Gross. I wasn't happy about it, either, and I was also confused—abuse? I wasn't sure where he saw it. But more and more I could feel my own anger as I wrote and read. I had already been Little Red Riding Hood, a helpless girl. And I had been Ariel, willing to give up anything to be loved. Now I felt like Dorothy, transported to a changed world, ready to go home, but unsure of what that meant.

Dorothy Comes Home from Work

This is how it begins—wind
whisking top hats, what's left of the roofs
of grayed barns, hurling it all into hayfields.

The stalks bent, roads scored like games of tic-tac-toe.

My husband and the dog perched on the seam
between the two husks of our double
wide, the velvet
sofa stained with ashes and stale piss.

I—applying Band-Aids, strip-searching
pubescent riffraff for Robitussin capsules, but then
we all had to hunker, keep our mouths between our knees.
The walls hissed. In the movies

cows rise up, sigh, float down safe and I think
this city has that same dumb-eyed grace. Motoring
back across the tracks I didn't fear I'd find
bodies. Worse, all my housework scattered on a field.

When I was young and white-skirted I wanted
more, more than plains rolling out like pie
crust. Places with cranes in the sky, steel
boned buildings rising.

I wanted my lips
to stand out like the brick courthouse
too strong to suffer from the kiss of any gust.
To come out in full-color, red

shoes, blue dress, none of that cropped
hair, black dress glamour, Lulu
Brooks tap-dancing across the screen silenced
by the whine of the film reel. And I came

home today to the whole house tipping to the still
ground, sofa slammed into the vanity.

The Cowardly Lion is the unemployed husband,
formerly a baker. Here, the men in my life blur together.
I think back to the pastry chef I was in love with; how
he showed me to knead bread. The husband's first poem
reads:

Unemployed

I would stand all morning
in the corner. Just the hum
of the halogen lights 'til 9.
Then, chefs ran
between the wire racks, red cutting
boards, stoves—waving scarred hands
with sauce on their cuffs. Pans clattered,
and I stood still shaping dinner
rolls. My motion—pull
off a piece, keep the palm

flat, roll the dough
against the wood—it forms
a taut skin, something to press against.

I can do more—
French bread, brioche, whole grain loaves
but the diner wants one thing: soft
globe to put his butter in. I'd come

home coated in flour, marks
from the day—red burn
across my chest from pressing
a sheet tray, hot and heavy,
against my uniform. But then, I was home
by 10 a.m. with all day to soak in Epsom,

wait for her to come back, prim
in her black pantyhose,
asking to be kneaded.

I'm writing more than anything else about my own
experience in a kitchen, standing alone listening to
'60s girl pop and making focaccia while everyone
around me moves. But in taking on a male perspective,
the metaphors get heavy-handed. "Soft globe to put
his butter in" is grossly ejaculatory, and "asking to

be kneaded" is a dumb and obvious pun to end the poem with. Reaching out to what I didn't know or understand—the perspective of the person who doesn't love me—stretched my capacity for empathy to its breaking point. I couldn't write from the voice of a speaker who wasn't myself and make him empathetic.

Beginning to work within the structure of a novel-in-verse, I tried to establish the conflict between these lovers. It was one almost every couple has faced: one party feels the other party is *bad at apologizing*.

Apologies

He bought a sunflower.
Doesn't smell sweet, all seeds,
and what does yellow mean, anyway—it doesn't
live two days without the sun.

Just like him, to give me something dead,
to have me watch while it dies again.
By my bed, its one eye cries petals
leaving just its fat green stem. All gifts open

empty space—discarded box, ripped envelope,
this vase—
But I want something

I can keep—like cacti.
They can live
a long time without sun, water, anyone's touch.

2. Apology (Unsent)

Don't you want me
to tell the truth?
Not much use to you
am I, waiting all day
to see your sad lips and full eyes.

You deserve a breast
of pheasant. A well whipped
serving of tiramisu. But I'm so tired
and we can't afford it. You deserve
flowers, a garden, and a fence.
But I can't help it — I need time
to miss you. I think of you so much
your face, sometimes,
is a disappointment.

Dorothy's words hearken back to my ex-boyfriend's
last "real" apology to me. The apologetic flower
always wilts and dies. Is this supposed to represent

the resentment of the wronged party drying up? The conflict drawing to a close? It seemed to me wrong that in order to apologize for hurting someone, you give him or her something that they must care for, watering and watching. This sunflower convinced me of this in its quick death, and here I memorialize it, as well as imagine a better alternative. The cactus might not be a go-to apology plant. But it does *live*; it can protect itself from poor care. It's clear enough that the speaker wants not only to have a cactus, but also to be a cactus: to thrive in spite of neglect, to keep unwelcome caresses away with barbs, to thrive with or without the sun.

*

The husband's unsent apology is so much worse than a sunflower. It is the admission that while he esteems his partner, and believes she deserves all the luxuries in the world, it is not his wish to give them to her. Her face, and really everything about her, is a disappointment.

This might seem a cruel and inaccurate portrait of the lover who fails to apologize. A projection from a young girl who believes that if she is not emotionally fulfilled by her partner, it is not simply because he doesn't know how to meet her needs; he doesn't want to, he refuses to, he wishes he could tell her how inadequate she is.

But in my grasping towards the emotions of all the men I'd dated, I still feel that I may have hit the nail on the head: I was a disappointment.

*

I posted another ad on craigslist. I can't remember what it said. I went on dates with two men; I got pho with both. There is nothing more difficult than making conversation with a stranger while slurping noodles. I walked down a cold, empty street to meet the first guy; he talked so little, and I so much, that I was exhausted and angry by the end of the night. And then shocked to see his text, *I had a great time*. I didn't respond. I met the second guy in a restaurant close to campus, and conversation came a little more easily. But he didn't kiss me on the first date, or the second, and I stopped responding to him, too.

*

It's interesting, too, that I identified myself with a woman who *worked hard*. Is that what I was doing?

Writing a poem every day, doing coursework, suturing my wounds and then breaking them open again? Perhaps I only wished to be working—to have some freedom from myself.

*

On New Year's Eve, I went home to my father's, then met up with Eloise and Daniel at a party in New York. How good to see my friends in a new context. I wore a pink dress in which I drank champagne and snorted ketamine.

I remember being in a room with Eloise, sitting on a bed, and suddenly screaming. Why? Someone had shown us his dick. Something about that.

Then she was crying. I would never know why.

The night went violet, then black. I woke up in the morning with my head throbbing. I went to a diner with my friends; I was too nauseous to eat anything but French fries.

I took a bus back to my dad's, my body giving off the fumes of all that I'd put in the night before. I felt sick, I felt tired; I fell asleep.

Three Versions of "Desire"

I applied to graduate school as I'd planned to do for so long. I wanted to be a *writer*. I was too young to know that "being a writer" at twenty-one did not mean I would *continue* to be a writer. That to make this identity permanent would require that I keep insisting on it, no matter how much I published, or where I worked, or when the last time I'd sat down with a pen or a laptop was.

But once I started an advanced workshop with a visiting instructor, I gave up on my novel-in-verse.

Higher education settings do not teach tenacity. A creative writing workshop is, in theory, a pluralistic model in which the many come together to help the one, in turn—as in a round robin. Each individual voice is supported, no matter how different they are. But in practice, these are highly structured and constrained spaces; members of the workshop have no relationship to each other prior to it. The workshop attempts to foster the kind of collaboration we associate with the surrealist movement, with 1920s Paris, with Gertrude Stein's salon. But as long as it is part of the hulking structure of the university, hierarchy reigns. The instructor's opinion is often the only one that anyone trusts.

In the spring, my instructor was unimpressed with my work. I abandoned my project completely in order to write work that she would praise. I was young. I had never received any real criticism about my writing, or anything else, for that matter, in an academic setting. Of "Apologies," she told me that the only interesting line was "What does yellow mean, anyway?" and that the rest of the poem could be scrapped. In other poems, there was even less to praise. Suddenly I felt that I hadn't ever written a single poem; I'd only generated a few clusters of words that could at best, at some distant point in the future, be woven into something worthy. I didn't know how to value my own work, or to listen to other input, or even to remember that my instructor had only seen a little glimpse into the project I had begun.

Of all the poems in the fragmented, fledgling novel-in-verse, she liked only one:

Laundry Day

When we met, he was drunk, I was young,
a red skirt, new blouse, I still remember

the night like any other.
Rain and the buds of things

glistened from the waxy leaves
of the cottonwood tree, skeletons
I used to climb. Some story line
had ripened in the branches.

He said you're so repressed I thought yes,
I am, had been waiting like paper
and he walked in like a branch breaking

so I saw the wick of my existence
thirst dried and stiff. I said yes.
The petals were white. Leaves trembled.

This poem seemed honest to her.

This is nothing like the way I actually lost my virginity—that happened on a hot summer night in Tompkins Square Park, where there are no cottonwood trees. But the feeling underneath it, the feeling that someone else could walk over to me, see to my core, and expose that there was nothing there—that had been true. I carried it with me still.

*

Although my breakup had been months ago, my romantic pain intensified. I felt like I was someone who was at my essence abandoned, alone, heartbroken. It was as if those emotions had long lived underneath the scrim of everything else I experienced in daily life—a warm ocean of feeling, and at the bottom, those pieces of thick, impenetrable ice. Occasionally, I swam too close to the bottom and felt their chill. Now I had forgotten how to swim upwards to gasp for air.

It was a frigid spring. Sometimes, just walking down the street to buy wine, my face hurt from the cold. Suddenly, I didn't want to go out much, didn't want to have my dinners with Daniel or even my breakfasts with the girls—I was ready for another period of retreating inwards. I was devastated by the news that my writing was flaccid. Just as I'd wanted to put as much distance between myself and my "fun" friends before, I did again. When Daniel texted to invite me over, I replied that I was busy. One night when he did manage to drag me to a party, he told me I was making a huge mistake, *ruining my life*, by refusing to go out, have fun. But I was resolute.

*

A friend of a friend was a student at the other local college, and we met up for coffee. He looked a lot like my ex, but a little slighter in build and with teeth a little crossed. He was studying classics and worked in the summer as a groundskeeper at the arboretum. After having stilted conversation over several cups of coffee, we headed to walk past the skeletons of trees. I had worn a coat that was too thin for the weather, and visibly shivered for twenty minutes. "Don't worry," I told him again and again, "I'll adjust." We took a long walk and talked about our relationships. He'd just stopped seeing the girl he dated in high school, but they'd been long distance for years and he'd never been that interested in her—he didn't think she was very smart.

We walked through the trees; I warmed up. We went to dinner at an Afghani restaurant and ate stewed pumpkin and meat, and then, spontaneously, went to the cinema downtown, where *Crazy Heart* was playing. (A pairing of words that already appeared throughout this writing, in my poems—a phrase I couldn't seem to escape.)

This sounds like the type of date that neither person wants to end. But what I felt was not that. In the movie theater, I couldn't get comfortable in my chair;

my back and neck hurt no matter how many times I shifted position. I *wanted* the feeling of wanting to be on the date, and that desire kept me in my seat. It brought me to his apartment, where there were teal walls, a record player, and a bottle of nice whiskey. As I sat on the bed he knelt on the floor, reaching up to cup my face in hands, telling me he was so surprised and happy to have met me. How excited he was that I was there.

The sex was bad, but I pretended to enjoy it, faking an orgasm and nuzzling my head on his chest afterwards. At least I was having sex again with someone who I could tell enjoyed it—someone who wanted me.

He tried to make me a breakfast of vegan scrambled eggs, but I told him I didn't eat tofu and needed to get cleaned up before class. He said he'd call me soon, come over to my place.

He didn't call me again. And I didn't want him to.

*

I began to write poems called "Desire."

Desire

When I sat at the center of the world
   I created, I didn't feel
like a gardener or god,
but like a child in a planetarium.
    My body
dark, surrounded by traces
of other bodies
    blown to stars.
Beautiful. I can't tell
if someone is sitting next to me—

The walls are sheets, the screen
for the projection,
    already set to move in circles.
The air is still. The floor is cold.
It all looks the same,
    my eyes open, closed.

I had only been to a planetarium of sorts as a kid in
Georgia. The cosmos was not projected onto a dome
that mimicked the shape of sky wrapping the earth.
There was simply a large room in the elementary
school in which the concrete brick of the wall was
swathed in sheets. The sheets created a kind of tent,

and we all sat on the floor looking at the crumpled stars. I felt so tired sitting in the dark, staring at the stars.

I conjure up this image, so particular to my own childhood, in imagining the present tense of my desire. I have created my own world, but I do not look upon it with pride, as does the gardener. I feel small—my own body obscure to me, and "other bodies blown to stars." The constellation Orion is defined by only seven points of light; looking at the sky, you have to know what you're searching for to find the shape of a man at all. He has no face; he is a gesture and a figure. This is what my desire was for: a person far away, completely abstract, and at the same time heavenly, beautiful.

This beauty is the beauty of the obscure, what is not readily seen or understood. The projections on the screens of the planetarium—the projection of my own desires onto my lover's starry body—look the same with my eyes open or closed. The projections are fantasies, and the planetarium is a kind of womb in which I am a child sitting amongst them, imagining them floating around me. My fantasies protect me from the reality just outside its walls, the chill of which creeps through the floor.

Writing this, it's clear I know desire is a projection. That does not make it any less potent, any less painful.

*

For my birthday, Daniel, Rachel, and I went to Boston to visit one of Daniel's friends. In turn, he took us to the gay club in his neighborhood. Unexpectedly, it was fetish night; Rachel and I were wearing black and were ready to go. Daniel had to take his pants off to gain entry. We went into the basement, where a few performers in steampunk lingerie hula-hooped on stage. Many women stood listlessly in corners, leaned against beams, wearing corsets and fishnets and boots. They had streaks of bright color in their hair and whips dangled from their loose grips. When I looked at them, they didn't look back at me; I did not belong.

At this point in my life I was certainly enjoying my pain, making no effort to escape it. I thought of the feeling of being "flayed," and after my experience with the graduate student two summers before I was curious to be hit again. Going to S&M night piqued that interest. I hoped someone would grab my hand, but this did not happen.

What did happen: we drank. A strange, shirtless man insisted on giving Rachel a massage. Daniel took that strange man's keys off the bar stool where he had left them, but eventually put them back. Daniel put his pants back on. We slept on air mattresses and sofas and couch cushions fitfully, then woke up with terrible hangovers. I told them over brunch that now, when I had drunk too much, lines from *The Waste Land* echoed in my head in Eliot's own scratchy, pretentious voice—"I was neither living nor dead, and I knew nothing."

They both laughed, even though they had never read *The Waste Land*.

Did my friends know how I was really feeling? This was a better birthday than I had had in years. I didn't want to ruin that closeness and joy with the revelation of my despair.

*

There are two other versions of desire.

Desire

Tonight, we are traveling
on the same road,
      but in separate vehicles—
      you, an hour ahead of me

so when I see snow
melting on my windshield,
        you have already gone
        through the tunnel,

        heard the radio's voice turn
        white. In the dark hum,
you've held your breath,
you've made a wish.

When night comes and the highway
lights up, the cars reduced

to winks of red and yellow,
you are back home
        standing coatless on the balcony
        with the potted geranium,

        looking at the sky. In the sky,
        the black clouds begin to part.

This is the only version of the poem that contains a "you"—and, moreover, a "we."

Driving was part of the tapestry of things I associated with my ex. I haven't loved anyone else who owns a car. In this ambiguous story, two people are driving in separate vehicles, but it remains unclear whether their destination is the same apartment, the same balcony with geraniums. The two cars suggest that they are sealed off from each other, isolated in their own pods, as are all of our lives. The speaker trails behind her beloved (although there is nothing but the title to suggest she desires him), and seems to have the worst end of the deal—she is surrounded by white snow, he is surrounded by the white noise of the radio—while he seems to have bypassed the downfall. He drives during daylight; she drives in the dark. He makes a wish; her wish goes unspoken. (Is it simply to be with him?) He looks at the sky as she squints at taillights.

The final image, though, belongs to both of them: the black clouds begin to part. Is this an image of hope, in which darkness lifts, the speaker arrives, and they kiss as the sun sets? Or is it an image in which the clouds are metaphors for the speakers: pulled apart by forces beyond their control, the sliver of the moon a cut that separates them from each other? None of these images, of course, is in the poem—none of them is even suggested. Really, all I can say is that this speaker seems jealous of her beloved's better luck.

By this point, I was jealous of my ex. Not jealous of the girls he dated or didn't date, but jealous of his

ability *to move on*. I was rehearsing the huge expen-
diture of energy from the previous year in everything
I wrote; I couldn't find any inspiration in my chilly
encounters with men, my days riding the bus with the
sky dark and my lips chapped.

I cut most of the poems from this period into
couplets:

> Will you hold what grows cold—
> the stump you've made of my heart?

*

> At night, I open the window and cry
> I, I, I out of it.

These lines are so melodramatic, filled with questions
and accusations; they reveal so much about me that is
not flattering, things I do not want heard or overheard.
This is why I've cut them down—but even the couplets
remain in my files, so clearly expressing a pain that I
couldn't discard. They do this work through figures
that don't quite make sense: moments of catachresis.
For example, "the stump you've made of my heart"
relies on a chain of metaphoric association. My heart
is like a tree: you've cut the tree down: my heart is

a stump. But this logic is missing from the couplet, missing from the poem. Really, it's missing from all love poems where the poet tries to reach out and touch someone with stanzas rather than fingertips.

I didn't know who I was trying to reach. I knew my ex had not wrought this wound. I talked about my feeling of loneliness with my therapist, the only thing as potent as my rage. Once again, I had to admit that I had been depressed for years. My first heartbreak had brought all my sadness back up into my lungs and life. It took on the form of longing most often, but it permeated everything. And eventually, I wanted to feel something else.

She urged me to at least practice self-care.

I dyed my hair back to red and started getting manicures. I couldn't think of anything else that would make me feel good. At least I looked a little bit more like myself.

*

Another version:

Desire

What was it?
Afterwards, I couldn't wait

to get home,
sit alone
like a cricket—listening
to the clicks of my wings

warmed in the light, held
safe in my own hard skin.

And, as I would a cricket,
I wanted to cage
and keep it with me—

set it on the windowsill to sing

as we both stare at the bright daffodils
through our pane of glass
until the sun sets, until our blood is cold.

I had started to write about desire as something
intensely private and strikingly inhuman. While there
is a desire for stars, for the planets themselves, and

also for nothing in particular in the first poem, here, the desire is to both be and capture an insect.

In early modern China, crickets were kept in beautiful, ornate cages; they were both pets and sources of song. This speaker, like a cricket, is cold-blooded; she wants to keep her desire in a cage next to her, separated from the world of light and growth, the world of daffodils, by a pane of glass.

The beloved is hardly in this poem; this is about the speaker and an erotic relationship to her own desire. The lover has faded further and further over the course of these three poems, has gone from a present pronoun and person to something implied, something that hovers *before*. I am not ashamed of the last poem; it seems to be the only one in which my sexuality is my own. But in letting go of "you" there is something lost: the cricket cage is also a metaphor for the poem itself, the thing that captures her desire, making it possible to observe. It is an ornament, a pretty thing, but it makes only the quietest of sounds.

Fisheyes

I got into graduate school. On my prospective student visit, I felt a whole world of potential was open to me: girls with cool haircuts welcomed me into their large apartments, and we smoked pot sitting on the floor. I met so many people in one weekend I thought my feeling of elation might expand and expand until my life was filled with people, parties, long talks about poetry. I could fill up on happiness, and then let my world contract again: once I was ready, I would reel in someone new.

*

When did I start seeing myself as bait?

When I was twelve, my mother and I walked into the parking lot of Ruby Tuesday's after dinner. "That man is looking at you," she said. I looked at the man, closer to her age, and got in the car. Face hot, I glanced through the window at the Movie Gallery across the street. I had walked through the "Adult" section by that time, trying not to look like I was looking at the titles of the DVDs hidden behind gray plastic.

I knew I was *jailbait*. I didn't know what to do with that knowledge as my body morphed and changed, growing upwards and outwards. When a few years later a man on St. Mark's Place asked me, "Is it red down there, honey?" I wanted to scream at him that I was fifteen, fifteen—he couldn't think of me like that. But I had learned it was better to walk away, and fast. Increasingly, I kept my eyes on the ground. I didn't want to know if anyone was looking.

In my twenties, I looked back up. I started to run on the elliptical. I bought dresses. I wore blush. For a few weeks that spring, the poet from the reading had forwarded me drafts of his poems about his longing for a young girl, told me that he played his flute and fantasized about my body. I knew, then, that I had achieved the power of temptation—that I both wanted this kind of feedback and was able to get it. I knew I could bait him.

But bait him to what end? Bait isn't, after all, just temptation. It comes with a catch—as with the nymph used to lure in fish. And I wasn't jailbait anymore.

*

To what end? To find a lover who could inspire *my*

next series of poems. To fall in love again. To stop hurting. To feel less ashamed about sex and myself.

My poems, as much as my actions, had shaped who I was: a girl who longed for an end to loneliness, and who was sure she'd find that if she could just find the right man and show him all of herself. I would use whatever tools I had: my words, my poems, my sad eyes peering into his, willing him to look deeper, deeper.

*

The summer before I moved, I traveled, trying to find what I was looking for.

First, I went to Europe for two weeks. I was a little scared to stay with Hannah in London. We were out of touch by then, but I knew that throughout her college years she'd been wilder than me. She wasn't plagued by the impulse that hit me again and again: to pull back from everything and sink into darkness. Instead, she partied all the time. I had hoped to have a low-key time in London, gathering some stillness and inspiration before I made the transition to a new city and program. But I knew that I'd be swept up in whatever her energy was.

I arrived on Derby Day, and although U.S. horse

racing isn't really celebrated in London, we nonetheless went to a cocktail bar in Hackney. We drank Mint Juleps out of copper cups, and I woke up on the couch the next morning feeling sick to death. We both vomited, taking turns in the bathroom. When we felt better, we ordered Indian food and started drinking wine.

After three glasses, I got my energy back: we decided to go to a rave—my first. I met a friend of Hannah's boyfriend, and he offered me ketamine. We danced, and when I broke a heel and became wobbly, he suggested we go back to his place.

When I whispered to Hannah that I was leaving, she laughed and winked. "You're still the same Charlotte," she said.

We went back to his flat and groped each other; he asked me if we could have sex without a condom. "American girls are usually up for anything," he told me. Knowing he'd been with other American girls, I insisted he use one.

Soon it became clear why he didn't want to: he had trouble staying hard, and the first condom fell off. I encouraged him to try again and asked what I could do. But as he stroked himself, eyes closed, I could see the frustration on his face. Light poured in through his thin white curtains: it was 6 a.m. and bright outside.

I told him I wanted to leave, and he seemed half-annoyed, half-relieved. He didn't offer to pay for the very expensive cab over to Hannah's.

When I arrived back, her boyfriend and his friends were smoking cigarettes in her living room, leaving me nowhere to sleep. I wanted to cry, but instead I smoked some pot and passed out in an armchair. When I woke up, I threw up again and again for the second morning in a row.

I was ashamed that, on the verge of moving forward, I was acting this way.

*

In graduate school, one of my instructors would tell me that my work was accomplished but "safe." And I agreed; I felt like I didn't know how to write something that "took risks."

But of course, the poems were about taking risks. Not formally, but with men who saw me as bait, men with whose lives I became ensnared, men who stalked me. I do not use these terms in a strictly metaphoric sense.

*

Fisheyes

The sky had been static for days.
When a leaf fell to the surface
of the pond, I thought it was the sun.

At night, the moon waxed. Then he came,
his face pale.

And what luck — he was a fisher,
I a fish—my gills
and flat black eyes asking
to be caught, for fingers
to stroke each scale and hook scar.

The water spilled
              back into itself. The pale orb
  rippled beneath us, for a moment—
              the first, the only. Then black.

How could you? I asked, then caught
              — still gilded —
my own face reflected in the glass.

On a camera, a fisheye lens creates a distorted
image. I see in this poem both an indictment of the

men who saw me as bait, as well as an image of myself so distorted as to make my face hot all over again. How could I have thought that?

I learned it from a larger mythology, the one that told me I was bait in the first place. I was an animal already pierced.

How could you? I ask the fisher, the one who has caught me and trapped me, but I see my own face. I have done this to myself. Again and again, I had gleefully dived into dangerous waters and blamed myself for the pain that followed.

What would it take to realize that I didn't like to be in pain?

*

Back at my dad's house for two months before my move to Providence, I looked half-heartedly for a summer job, but spent most of my time surrounded by sheets of my printed-out poems. What was good? What was salvageable?

Everything seemed to be about heartbreak. Finally, I could wake up in the morning without thinking about my ex-boyfriend, but when I looked back on the past year of work, it was hard to find a line of verse not haunted by him. I wanted to untangle my story from his, to find a new subject. But my mind was blank.

To get a break, I took the bus from my dad's house to the Port Authority, and then took the L to Daniel's apartment. Almost as soon as I arrived, I cried. What was wrong? "I don't know what I'm doing with my life," I said. I had a clearer path than anyone, my friends assured me. I was still in school! Everything else would fall into place. In the meantime, I should just enjoy my summer of freedom. We should go to a party.

We did, and there I met another man.

*

Almost every time I saw him, he gave me molly. That party was the first time: drunk on a roof in Bushwick, I sat looking into my phone. He came up and asked if we'd met before. We hadn't, but I didn't mind being flirted with; attention always made me feel better. I introduced myself the way I always did, and he asked if I was bored. I was, so I took a little piece of tissue filled with white powder; it looked like the Bang Snap fireworks I'd thrown on the ground as a kid. I swallowed it with my Miller Lite.

A few hours later, he told me he had been looking

for someone like me—someone who could help him with *his* writing. He had great ideas and he needed to share them, he said. Ideas about a new way of life and being. I thought he was as high as I was; I laughed accommodatingly.

Soon we were kissing, and then we were stumbling down to the host's apartment so that I could use the bathroom. He knew the guy who lived there from high school, the same guy Daniel knew from college. It turned out we had some acquaintances in common. This made me feel safe.

He knew his way around. The host's bedroom was lofted over the kitchen, accessible only by a rope ladder. Did I want to see?

I did. I crawled up, him behind me, and when I arrived, I rolled my body over onto the fluffy lambswool carpeting, my heart beating in my ears. He rolled on top of me, and we kissed. He began to fumble under my skirt, stroking my thighs, and I didn't stop him; I would wait until he asked about the condom, I thought. But he didn't ask. He put himself inside me, and high, I thought, *Fuck, that's another one to my number*, angry at myself for failing to say anything before I took the molly, before we went down to the apartment, before we went up to the lofted room.

I tried to fake enjoyment. Rolling, I felt the borders

of myself hazy and sparkly; it was like I wasn't even there.

When we returned to the roof, he put his arm around my shoulders, already possessive. *He really seems to like you*, a few friends said, as if I should be grateful for that. I would hear that about him for years: "It sounds like at least you found a guy who liked you!" As if that were all that any woman wants or deserves.

*

When he called the next day and asked if I wanted to go on a date, I said yes. If we had sex twice, maybe it wouldn't be as shameful a mistake.

There were many warning signs. He talked again about his revolutionary ideas, even while sober, or what passed as sober for him: they all involved self-transcendence through drugs. *How many does he take?* I wondered. I didn't care, though, when he paid for my dinners, when he gave me molly again and again. When we fucked, surprisingly, it did feel good, most of the time. Sometimes, he pushed me to do something I didn't want to, and then I said no again and again until he relented and I cried.

He asked why I was crying so much. He started telling me that he loved me, that he didn't want to hurt me. We'd only known each other for two weeks.

In most of the relationships I'd pursued, I felt like I was trying to convince the man to love me—to give me one more night, one more chance, to prove that I could be fun and interesting and kind and wonderful. This time, though, I didn't have to make any effort; he was devoted from the beginning. I didn't know what to think about this. I didn't love *him*, I knew that much. Our first sexual encounter colored everything in a complicated way. I felt a mixture of fear and revulsion and confusion and pleasure when I thought of him. Now I was saying yes—or, when I needed to, no—but that didn't erase what had happened. And the drugs made it all the more confusing.

Another aspect: he seemed genuinely hurt when I cried. He told me he loved me again and again; that he'd never felt like this. He wanted so much from me, and I got to choose how to respond. Now, he wanted to make things official, to be my boyfriend.

Several friends thought I should continue with the bit. Why not? If he were crazy, at least that was something to write about.

I hadn't told them what he'd done. A part of me thought that if he were my boyfriend, he couldn't have assaulted me; I would somehow have offered consent retroactively, and then I wouldn't have to see myself as a victim for any longer.

*

He wanted me to write a poem about him. I didn't. I couldn't.

*

Poetry was perhaps a good anchor for creating a sense of self, the belief that I was someone with power and purpose. But it also enabled me to romanticize the worst relationships I had even been in, to prolong pain in order to produce verse. I sought out intense experience from many motivations and justified it all as worth it—as long as it led to another poem. But now, that wasn't working, and the other results were becoming unbearable.

*

At my first graduate school party, everything was surreal. In a philosophy student's backyard and small living room, first-years sipped from a keg, sizing each other up. I was drunk, teetering on my heels. But I still noticed that one guy was *very* drunk, banging on the bathroom door, trying to get someone to let him in. A half-hour later, I saw him hitting his head against the frame of the apartment door. I alerted my new acquaintance, Hal. Hal and I watched as he hit his head harder and harder, starting to bleed. He was blocking the door, and no one could go in or out. I wanted to cry. I suddenly felt too sober. Other men started to approach him: *What's up? Calm down, buddy.* Soon they were trying to tear him away from the wall, splotched with red. He was screaming.

I asked Hal to leave with me, to walk through the city with which I was still unfamiliar. We went to his house and smoked a bowl. I told him about my predicament: I was beginning this new life, but I still had a boyfriend—a man I'd met six weeks ago—who thought he was deeply in love with me. Now, with the space of a week between us, I wasn't even sure I liked him. But I didn't know how to end it. "You're in a drug-based relationship," he commented. I realized he was right. I was starting to see that I didn't, hadn't ever wanted anything to do with this man. Hal walked me home.

I woke up the next day and made the phone call. I lay on my floor and cried as he told me, long-distance, what a terrible person I was. How manipulative I was being, testing his love. How selfish I was to act like this when we belonged together.

He asked me what this was really about.

I didn't tell him that I didn't really even like him. But I did insist that our first encounter wasn't consensual.

"Are you fucking kidding me?" he asked. "That's a lie," he said. "You were wearing leopard print. You wanted it. You enjoyed it. And you love me."

I hung up.

*

The next week, I turned some old poems in to workshop. My classmates talked about the word choice. What kind of leaf fell? Could it at least have a color? It is better to give a fish a species than to simply call it a fish—maybe an angler? Maybe an angelfish?

I returned home to find my porch littered with things. A potted plant; flowers in a vase. In the rush of feeling, I did not observe their species or kind. I left them all on the porch and went upstairs feeling like I might vomit. I'd somehow brought up a greeting card with me.

In it held an invitation to meet him at a nearby restaurant. He'd be there all night, he wrote. I texted him to leave me alone. He began to text me over and over again. Threats and bribes and declarations of love. I shook all over. I couldn't find a way to block his number.

I called Hal, and we went out to dinner. I confided in him: I wanted nothing more than for this person to go away, to leave me in my fragile peace, to stop telling me I was beautiful, horrible, abusive, his great love.

Hal asked if I wanted to spend the night. No, I wanted to be in my own bed, to pretend like things were normal. I went home and left the plants to die on the porch in the autumn cold.

*

High in the summer, my body slick with longing, I didn't listen when he said, "I want to found a new religion." I laughed when he said, "I know how to use drugs to make life nothing but good." I shrugged when he told me our meeting was meant to be. To make sense of what had happened—how he'd taken power over me—I had taken as much power as I could over him by framing him in my mind as ridiculous; silly; even harmless.

But finally, I saw he had manipulated me every way he knew how. And that I wanted my body—my life—to be my own again.

He sent texts for another twenty-four hours; I stopped responding. Then, finally, he was ready to leave: he told me he'd leave me "my stuff" in my mailbox. That meant a pair of dirty underwear, a copy of *The Autobiography of Red*. That he had driven four hours with these things in a bag, that he had put them in my mailbox, terrified me. That I never again wanted to read my favorite book disgusted me. That he texted again with fury when he found the dead flowers on the porch scared me more. I could stop texting, but he knew where I lived; he could stand outside my door, drop by, any time. That he existed and sought me out—I could barely bear to think about it. I wanted to disappear, or for him to disappear, or to go into a coma until the situation was resolved.

I was sure he would be back.

*

I had felt like bait; I had presented myself that way in my poetry. This was what it felt like to be caught: bees took up residence in my chest and never stopped buzzing, crawling up into my throat and down into my belly. I tried to hold my breath to kill them, but they lived. Staying alive with them inside of me became my only work. There was no point in writing any more. There was nothing to write about. I led myself from place to place. I didn't think about what I wanted, what I was aiming for. "Stay in the present," my yoga teacher told me. My therapist gave more specific advice: run your hands under hot water; snap a rubber band on your wrist; list five things you can see, hear, feel—then four, then three, then two—then see how you feel. No better? Start again.

*

I kept a diary. I named it after one of my favorite books of poetry: Galway Kinnell's *The Book of Nightmares*. In my favorite section of the book, a woman fears she has been possessed by a demon:

Dear Galway,

I have no one to turn to because God is my enemy. He gave me lust and joy and cut off my hands. My brain is smothered with his blood. I asked why should I love this body I fear. He said, It is so lordly, it can never be shaped again-dear, shining casket. Have you never been so proud of a thing you wanted it for your prey? His voice chokes my throat. Soul of asps, master and taker:

he wants to kill me. Forgive my blindness.

Yours, in the darkness,
Virginia

I felt like Virginia in the darkness, possessed by forces beyond my control, unable to speak. I was also having terrible nightmares.

In one, I went back to the house I grew up in, the house in Georgia. I entered in disguise to try and sneak my little brother out. But my mother knew who I was immediately and attacked me with knitting needles; I tried to run away, but I tripped. She grabbed me by the ankle and pierced me through the foot.

I dreamt of my aunt, my father's sister, who had died. In my dream, she was alive, and no one else knew. As we sorted through her bedroom, my father kept trying to give me her shoes. When I left the room, she came out and led me into the closet, which was deep and cavernous. She tried to give me a beautiful pair of heels, but they didn't fit.

I dreamt I was going to practice yoga with my dad. He wore sweatpants. We had all forgotten yoga mats and were embarrassed. Some people were doing the sequence on towels—I probably needed one too; I had my period. While I was trying to start my sun salutations, the room suddenly got dark. I couldn't concentrate; next to my mat was a bag of insects trying to crawl out. I bled everywhere. Were they attracted to *me*?

I dreamt that Daniel and I were going on vacation. We had driven a long way. We showed up to a ballroom, a festival, and the first room they showed us to sleep in was a long corridor, very narrow, like a cave. Someone would have to crawl into the depths to sleep and wouldn't be able to get out over the other person. We were shown a variety of other sleeping options, many of them coffin-like, confined.

I dreamt I couldn't wake up.

I dreamt I woke up only to find myself blind in one eye and unable to speak.

Le Silence de Charlotte

My suspicions had been right; it was not over. He looked for me on OKCupid. He sent me little emails, pretending to casually check in. He came back in November. I talked to the campus police and they sent him a letter of warning.

But nothing could give me relief.

I learned how to create the same fear in myself again and again, to dive into the sticky abyss of anxiety. I saw a strange car outside my apartment—I panicked. I saw someone who looked like him—I panicked. Sitting at home, in bed, going over unreturned text messages and e-mails, over school assignments, over whether or not to go to this place or that place—I panicked. "This is hyper-vigilance," my therapist told me. "This is a common side-effect of PTSD." I repeated this to myself. My body was constantly under strain, my nerves fraying. I sobbed every time I talked to someone about my feelings.

I had responsibilities. I had to *teach* while feeling like that. Luckily, I knew by then how to shove everything down.

If my professors noticed, they didn't say anything.

*

For every modern poet who jumped off a boat or bridge, there is another who simply stopped writing. John Keats abandoned his epic poem *Hyperion*. George Oppen was for twenty-five years unsure that poetry could serve political praxis. Laura (Riding) Jackson renounced poetry as too artificial and formal for the task of giving shape to selfhood. Arthur Rimbaud stopped writing at the age of twenty-one, entering a period called "le silence de Rimbaud" in which he became a colonist rather than a poet.

In *The Hatred of Poetry*, Ben Lerner argues that poetry is "impossible," that individual poems can never live up to the task of Poetry writ large: to provide both perfect aesthetic enjoyment as well as confirmation of our shared humanity. But I wonder whether it is really the impossibility of the art that leads so many poets to put down their pens. Perhaps they have simply lost the unselfconsciousness and faith in the written word needed to 'be' a poet. Or perhaps it is 'being a poet' that proves impossible.

*

Anne Carson writes that for the Greek poets, "change of self is loss of self."

When my idea of myself as a writer crumbled, I felt like I was no one. I became aware, hyper-critical, of the way I presented myself to the world. I had learned at a young age that it was safest to hide my distress. By the time I was an adolescent, the performance had become a personality. I was catty; I approached life with an eye-roll. Sometimes, in a moment of real pain, that all unraveled, but even my occasional bounds of public misery seemed melodramatic rather than real. Artistic, even. Part of the show.

Poetry became a way to both divert and perform pain: to hold it at a distance, to make it something else. It could help me no longer. Now, there was so much I couldn't put into words: the dark knots of feeling I tried to shove down each time they bubbled up, and the consequent sense that I was always thwarting myself, in writing and in life. I didn't know how to tell my friends that I feared I truly was "unbearable." Or that I worried the rage my ex-boyfriend had seen in me—*you're just like your mother*—might really be there. I didn't know how to describe what it felt like to have once perceived myself as creative and talented, and then to experience the loss of that identity.

But I knew I couldn't express it in poems, those little stylized little fragments of the whole. I had to learn to hold more of the truth in my own mind.

*

Foucault's late-career introduction of writing as a tool for the care of the self is an attempt to find a space for personal action under what we might call unbearable conditions. In most of his work, it seems that the individual cannot escape the apparatus of power. Rules and moral codes that once belonged to institutions have, over centuries, found a way to weave their way into individual consciousness. Power itself, inhuman and lively, is yielded by various actors until every sphere of life is constrained. The structures we live in are reflected in, imprinted on, the canvas of our minds: we police ourselves. Even the work we try to do as *self-care,* submitting to psychoanalysis and therapy, is another way that power first compels the individual to confess, and then to conform.

In his late writing, Foucault suggests a way out for the individual if not for the collective. Yes, we must struggle for liberation from systems of oppression. But, "this practice of liberation is not in itself sufficient to define the practices that will still be needed if this people, this society, and these individuals are to be able to define admissible and acceptable forms of existence or human society."

We must also seek freedom—within the self and from our own appetites, desires, and fears.

*

If the world is unbearable—its people have hurt you, its insects and animals and plants have hurt you, the things you have learned have hurt you—the only retreat is going further inwards. Down and down, into whatever corner of the self is uncontaminated, joyful, spacious. Concentrate on that corner, and perhaps you can cultivate it: breathe into it, water it, weed it, hope it grows a little more. Go there, to that tiny garden, and nourish yourself on its fruits. At the end of yoga class, you might hear, *You can go to this place whenever you need to*, this place inside: dark and hidden, fertile and safe.

And perhaps this place becomes a notebook. Perhaps when you open it, you plant seeds. When you hold it, you feel lighter. Perhaps you hold it out to someone else, and in the light, it thrives. You both feel a bit better, having shared, having seen and been seen.

But for me, writing no longer granted that. Poetry

no longer served as that space.

*

In an essay called "Looking at the Stars Forever," literary critic Rei Terada examines Keats's unfinished *Hyperion*. When writing it, Keats had witnessed the failure of the French revolution; collective action did not transform France, England, or the West, much less the material conditions of his own life. In her essay, Terada considers the gesture of *stopping*, giving up, abandoning one's work, as well as the imagery of the poem, in which Hyperion gazes up at the "same, bright patient stars" with unblinking eyes. In a subsection titled "How to Adjust to the Dark," she argues that Keats' abandonment is one way to adjust to political realities—and perhaps a more courageous gesture than writing that tries to make sense of a catastrophic world, to normalize it.

What good could poetry do for Keats anymore? By simply stopping, he presented another option: "No longer enduring, no longer converting dismemberment into being."

*

I had stopped trying to put the fragments of myself into new wholes. Instead, I brought my old little lyrics to workshop, listened as my instructor and colleagues recommended I swap out the word "little" for "small," and other minor adjustments to a way of thinking and writing that I was beginning to doubt made any sense at all. I was teaching creative writing to undergraduates, feeling like a fraud. I tried method after method recommended by my new therapist and the half-dozen books I bought on craft: erasure poems, getting inspiration from tarot cards, meditating to open my body to the flow of universal energy and just let the verse come through.

None of it felt right.

How
to
Adjust
to
the
Dark

Some years are filled with energy and momentum and accomplishment; others are about survival. I accepted this reality, and things improved. Or, I should say, I improved things for myself: I wove strands between myself and new people, new pursuits.

As usual, new problems arose. After a year of friendship, I was falling in love with Hal.

In the fall, we had watched *Gossip Girl* together, smoking pot and laughing about other graduate students, this silly life of the mind we were trying to lead. I did not want to break this fragile happiness with my desire, did not want the ease and joy to be polluted by the feelings that came up again: fear that I would ruin everything, or that he would. That what had been sweet would become sour. Fear that I would begin to feel feelings too big for my body again.

In the spring, I talked to Rachel about it on the phone, the way it thrilled me when our legs brushed up against each other. The way he never tried to kiss me, although I could tell by the look in his eyes that he wanted to. "What do you have to lose?" she asked.

Everything. This one person who made me feel safe,

who didn't think I was crazy or making it up that I felt watched, unsafe. He didn't even mind when I started to cry on a trip to the grocery store together. Instead, he picked up a banana in the produce section and cradled it to his ear. "Ring, ring."

"What are you doing?"

"The banana phone is ringing. Are you going to pick it up?"

"How?"

"Just pick it up."

I picked up a banana. He talked into his. "Hey. Charlotte. How's it going?"

Despite myself, I started to laugh. And then we bought ice cream and made banana splits.

But maybe it wasn't real. If it were real, shouldn't I be able to write about it?

In the summer, we took walks together every day. On one, we passed an elementary school. It was already early evening, the sky pink around us. The school's playground was vacated, save for a lone tennis ball. He gave it a kick, and we watched it head towards a set of sidewalk cellar doors. He pulled one open.

"Should we go down?" He asked.

"Do you think we're allowed to?"

He took out his cell phone, turned on the flashlight, and down we went.

How to Adjust to the Dark

We go through the door we're not
supposed to. The coos
of pigeons sound

down the stairs, into the black.
Beneath the school a lone chair stands
at the corner of every corridor,

lit up by the flashlight in your hand.
You make it your dark space—
so back into the coves

we go. Dirt on my coat.
Broken into, offered up:
hunks of metal, unhinged doors.

I ask my heart to stop.
A ladder leads
to the place where all

the balls from the schoolyard fall;
you hand me one

my hands still warm from the night before
now dirt stained, too.

It was light out.
And the door was open.

It was the last poem I ever wrote.

*

I left my MFA program without a degree. I started
a different graduate program, but I kept teaching
creative writing to high school students in the summer.
I introduced Hal to Rachel and Daniel and Eloise,
and even Hannah. No one told me he was bad for me.
We were engaged, then we were married.

I still couldn't write. Perhaps tethering myself to a
man instead of my craft meant that I was no longer
an artist. I had made and unmade myself through the
medium of verse; now, having abandoned it, it could
be that the identity I had once wanted *more* than
kindness, *more* than love, was now lost to me forever.

But in reading everything from fortune cookies to
literary theory, I saw that I should go back. Perhaps I
could even begin again.

Re-reading my old poems, I thought for a while

I was going inwards, uncovering layer after layer of belief and personality and trope and meaning. And I thought when I got to the end, I'd learn some kind of truth about myself: something new, something other than what had been told to me by therapists and psychiatrists and friends and my dad. Something worth sharing with others. This little light of mine.

I did learn something. I wanted to destroy everything that made those poems possible. Everything I was taught about what it means to be a writer, an artist, and a woman. Everything I was told about what it means to be traumatized, and depressed, and diagnosed. None of these beliefs made me happy—they just made poems. And knots in my chest, my calves, the back of my throat.

*

I started asking new questions—in the morning, in the bathtub, in the middle of the night. *What else is in me, around me? Can I become aware of more than the bees in my chest—can I feel my whole body? There it is.*

What else is there? The room I'm in, the cat underneath the sofa.

What else can I feel? The whole building?

The loam and lizards underneath the house, the

mosquitos in the air, the rain falling on treetops?

What else? The whole neighborhood, with people drunk and asleep and crying and happy? The cats prowling the streets, the sun's heat stuck in the air?

What else? The city, its tallest buildings and its ruins, its young and old, its pet cats and its cars?

What else? The ocean to the east, with knotted dead zones and all that lives around them?

What else?

Further, further. Into the sky; into the earth. Into the dark; into the light.

Now how do you feel?

Now why do you write?

To ask a question: what else is possible? And to ask for help in answering it.

Works Consulted

Auden, W.H. *The Complete Works of W. H. Auden: Prose, Volume II 1939-1948*. Princeton University Press, 2002.

Barthes, Roland. *A Lover's Discourse*. Hill and Wang, 1977.

Bynum, Caroline Walker. *Holy Feast, Holy Fast*. University of California Press, 1988.

De Man, Paul. "Autobiography as De-Facement." *The Rhetoric of Romanticism*. Columbia University Press, 1984.

Carson, Anne. *Eros the Bittersweet*. Dalkey Archive, 1998.

Eliot, T.S. "The Wasteland." *The Wasteland and Other Poems*. Faber & Faber, 1972.

Foucault, Michel. "Technologies of the Self." *Ethics: Subjectivity and Truth*. The New Press, 1984.

—"Self-Writing." *Ethics: Subjectivity and Truth*.

Freud, Sigmund. *On Narcissism*. 1914.

Kinnell, Galway. *The Book of Nightmares*. Houghton Mifflin, 1971.

Lerner, Ben. *The Hatred of Poetry*. Farrar, Straus and Giroux, 2016.

Sappho. *If Not, Winter*. Trans. Anne Carson. Vintage Books, 2003.

Terada, Rei. "Looking at the Stars Forever." *Studies in Romanticism*, vol 50, issue 2, Summer 2011, pp. 275-309.

White, Gillian. Lyric Shame: The "Lyric" *Subject of Contemporary American Poetry*. Harvard University Press, 2014.

Acknowledgments

Thanks to Joshua Bohnsack, Joe Demes, and Nathan Stormer for believing in this book and bringing it into the world, and to Erik Intlekofer, for his careful edits to the poems contained in this volume and Don't Nod.

To Natalie Adler, Cameron Blaylock, John-David Brown, Laura Janka, Steven Thompson, Alissa Trepman, Tim Wojcik, Veronica Wong, and Jordan Zandi for their support of me and my writing in its various iterations and stages.

To my friends and colleagues at Boston University and Baruch College for feedback and insights that helped shape the poetry and prose in this book.

To the editors at *The Cimarron Review*, *Crab Creek Review*, *The Battered Suitcase*, *Flatmancrooked*, and *TriQuarterly* for publishing early versions of the poems and chapters contained herein.

To Elizabeth Ellen, Lindsay Lerman, and Bud Smith for generously lending their words in support of mine.

To Shannon McLeod, for her constant companionship alongside the journey to publication.

To my parents, Lee van Laer and Neal Harris, for their love and encouragement, and to my grandmother Helen, who is no longer with us, but always believed that I had a book in me.

To my cat Gus, and in loving memory of his best friend Toby.

To my partner in all things, Steven Swarbrick—my love and light.

Rebecca van Laer's writing appears in *TriQuarterly*, *Joyland*, *Columbia Journal*, *The Florida Review*, *Salamander*, *Hobart*, *Monkeybicycle*, the *Ploughshares* blog, *Electric Literature*, and elsewhere. She holds a PhD in English from Brown University, where she studied queer and feminist autobiography. She lives in the Hudson Valley.

Long Day Press

New & Forthcoming Titles

Whimsy
Shannon McLeod
Novella
ISBN: 9781950987108 • $14

Rain Revolutions
Bessie Flores Zaldívar
Stories
ISBN: 9781950987177 • $14

Milkshake
Travis Dahlke
Novella
ISBN: 9781950987214 • $16

The Everys
Cody Lee
Screenplay
ISBN: 9781950987153 • $18

LongDayPress.com @LongDayPress